"Psychologically complex and suspenseful until the literal last sentence, [*Mouth to Mouth*] uses every word of its 200 or so pages to the fullest."
—NPR'S *POP CULTURE HAPPY HOUR*

"Wilson is a first-rate yarn spinner. . . . [A] sly and energetic novel."
—*THE WASHINGTON POST*

"Incredibly taut, with funny and brilliantly described scenes of the Los Angeles art world . . . [*Mouth to Mouth* is] powered by a kind of ominous propulsive forward momentum right up until the very end, which is unexpected and inevitable, as all the best endings are." —*VANITY FAIR*

"By the end of the slim volume Antoine Wilson has made sure to wallop the reader with the realization that the story has been eerier than they ever realized." —*ENTERTAINMENT WEEKLY*

"An elegantly told and supremely gripping tale of serendipity and deception . . . Delivers a brilliant ending that will leave you guessing about everything that came before." —*VOGUE*

"*Mouth to Mouth* is the best book I've read in ages. Narratively ingenious, delicately written, intriguingly plotted, it is literature of the highest quality." —ANDREW SEAN GREER, **Pulitzer Prize–winning author of *Less***

"A slow burn à la Patricia Highsmith that keeps us terminally off balance." —*OPRAH DAILY*

"Sleek, swift, and graceful—an agile novel of ideas with unexpectedly sharp teeth." —LAUREN GROFF, **author of *Matrix***

"A gloriously addicting tale of decisions and deception." —*BUZZFEED*

"A taut, heady thriller." —*LOS ANGELES TIMES*

PRAISE FOR *MOUTH TO MOUTH*

LONGLISTED FOR THE SCOTIABANK GILLER PRIZE

NAMED A BEST BOOK OF THE YEAR BY
NPR, *VOGUE*, AND *ESQUIRE*

ONE OF BARACK OBAMA'S FAVORITE BOOKS OF THE YEAR

"[An] enthralling literary puzzle . . . Wilson is a gorgeous writer, pulling you in and compelling you to keep reading. The story, and the story-within-the-story—the twists and turns, the attention lavished on motivation and emotion, the efforts to rationalize or at least explain strange or unsavory behavior—recall the cool prose of Paul Auster . . . This powerful, intoxicating book's greatest tension is that we have no idea where it is heading, right up to the shocking final sentence."

—Sarah Lyall, *The New York Times*

"Propulsive, slim, and inventive . . . *Mouth to Mouth* [is a] Russian doll of a novel."

—Sloane Crosley, *Departures*

"*Mouth to Mouth* is that rarity, a perfect narrative machine, working by its own laws. The cool nervous clarity of the prose enmeshes the reader in a trap of complicity, one snapping shut on narrator and reader at the same instant. Bravo."

—Jonathan Lethem, author of *The Fortress of Solitude*

"[A] propulsive . . . page-turner . . . A deliciously nasty morality play in the guise of a thriller."

—*Kirkus Reviews*

"Oh, to have an afternoon free and to have not yet read *Mouth to Mouth*! . . . [A] sleek train crash of a novel."

—Maris Kreizman, *Vulture*

"[A] shifty work of psychological suspense . . . There's plenty of satisfaction in watching the characters navigate the blurred line between plausibility and truth."

—*Publishers Weekly*

"Reminiscent of the cult classic film *My Dinner with Andre* . . . Antoine Wilson's slyly disturbing and shrewd novel presents two college acquaintances who unexpectedly cross paths at an airport almost 20 years later . . . Stopping isn't an option."

—*Shelf Awareness*

"The sinewy and mesmerizing narrative of Antoine Wilson's masterful novel aims straight at the heart of the mythologized self, which, like the world of art and commerce that provides the story's backdrop, trades in all forms of performance and deception. Not unlike the novel itself, which asks us to believe and doubt and then believe again within the space of a single sentence. Wilson's on a high wire and he never makes a wrong move."

—Marisa Silver, author of *Little Nothing* and *The Mysteries*

"Antoine Wilson has written a spellbinding novel of laser-like insight and exquisite technique that reveals how stories can function to conceal other stories. I read this book in one rapturous sitting, jotting down line after line, riveted until the final shocking, clarifying sentence."

—Sarah Manguso, author of *Ongoingness*

"Compulsively readable. This austere and addictive novel interrogates the very nature of identity, destiny, and storytelling."

—Adam Johnson, Pulitzer Prize–winning author of *The Orphan Master's Son*

"Antoine Wilson has written a stunner of a novel. *Mouth to Mouth* shook and thrilled me from the first page to the last."
—Daniel Alarcón, author of *The King Is Always Above the People* and *At Night We Walk in Circles*

"This book might be sold as a psychological thriller, but it's really—and, if allusions can be spoilers, then this might be a big one—a Gen-X Greek revenge fantasy. Gnarly, dude."
—*Washington Independent Review of Books*

"[A] roller-coaster ride of a novel."
—*Alta*

"Wilson chronicles the aftermath of a lifesaving rescue of an art dealer—and the twisting corridors of power and identity that this novel's protagonist ends up hurtling down in its wake."
—*Vol. 1 Brooklyn*

"A memorable novel . . . Masterfully written [and] undeniably compelling."
—*The Suburban*

"A compulsively readable narrative up to the very end."
—*Los Angeles Daily News*

"A storytelling triumph . . . This novel is intentional, focused and expertly delivered."
—*The Michigan Daily*

"I myself loved this riveting and smart novel. And: the perfect ending will make you gasp."
—Edan Lepucki, *The Millions*

"Tightly coiled . . . *Mouth to Mouth* delivers a tidy story that also will make readers wonder how much of Jeff's story is true and how much is just a good yarn."

—*South Florida Sun Sentinel*

"A fascinating contemporary twist on the classic 'as told to' novel . . . Mesmerizing."

—Janet Fitch, author of *Chimes of a Lost Cathedral*
and *Paint It Black*

MOUTH TO MOUTH

A NOVEL

ANTOINE WILSON

AVID READER PRESS

New York   London   Toronto   Sydney   New Delhi

Avid Reader Press
An Imprint of Simon & Schuster, Inc.
1230 Avenue of the Americas
New York, NY 10020

First Avid Reader Press trade paperback edition January 2023

AVID READER PRESS and colophon are trademarks of Simon & Schuster, Inc.

For information about special discounts for bulk purchases, please contact Simon & Schuster Special Sales at 1-866-506-1949 or business@simonandschuster.com.

The Simon & Schuster Speakers Bureau can bring authors to your live event. For more information or to book an event, contact the Simon & Schuster Speakers Bureau at 1-866-248-3049 or visit our website at www.simonspeakers.com.

Interior design by Carly Loman

Manufactured in the United States of America

10 9 8 7 6 5 4 3 2 1

Library of Congress Cataloging-in-Publication Data has been applied for.

ISBN 978-1-9821-8180-2
ISBN 978-1-9821-8181-9 (pbk)
ISBN 978-1-9821-8182-6 (ebook)

To Chrissy

1

I sat at the gate at JFK, having red-eyed my way from Los Angeles, exhausted, minding my own business, reflecting on what I'd seen the night before, shortly after takeoff, shortly before sleep, something I'd never seen before from an airplane.

I'd been on the left side of the plane, and we'd gone south over the ocean, accident of fate, affording me a panoramic view of the city at night: amber streetlights dotting neighborhoods; red-stripe, white-stripe garlands of freeway traffic; mysterious black gaps of waterways and parkland. Then a small burst of light, not at ground level but above it. Another burst of light, streaks opening like a flower in time lapse. A fireworks show. I watched the little explosions until we penetrated the cloud layer.

It wasn't a holiday.

I was thinking about how a sight that might consume our attention completely on the ground could, from another perspective, barely register as a blip on an enormous field, when I heard a name over the PA.

"Jeff Cook," the agent said. "Please check in at the counter for Gate Eleven."

A common enough name, but it piqued my attention. I had known a Jeff Cook once, at UCLA, almost twenty years earlier. Looking up, I saw a handsome man in his forties striding toward the counter. He was dressed in a sharp blue suit, no tie, glasses with transparent Lucite frames. Expensive leather loafers. He said his name to the gate agent and slid his boarding pass and identification across the counter. While she clicked away at the noisy keyboard, he leaned slightly on the handle of his fancy hard-shelled roll-aboard suitcase.

From where I sat near the gate, I could examine this Jeff Cook closely, in profile. I had all but determined that he wasn't the Jeff

Cook I'd known and was going to turn my attention elsewhere, when he looked in my direction. I knew those high, broad cheek-bones and that penetrating gaze.

It was he. But Jeff had had famously long, dark flowing hair, not this cropped salt-and-pepper business. Plus he'd put on weight, become more solid in the way so many of us did after college, continuing to grow into manhood long after we thought we'd arrived.

We hadn't been friends, exactly, barely acquaintances, but Jeff was one of those minor players from the past who claimed for himself an outsize role in my memories.

During my freshman year I experienced a series of encounters, if they could even be called that, in various locations on and off campus, with a fellow student who had, for some reason or another, caught my attention. With his cascading hair and distinctive features, he was hard to miss, a sort of thrift-store Adonis, and he carried himself with the quiet confidence of an upperclassman. We didn't cross paths so much as he would just pop up from time to time, at a table in the corner of a coffee shop, wandering around a protest for the first Gulf War, or—most randomly—lit up by my car's reverse lights as I backed out of a friend's driveway one night. Every sighting of this mystery man yielded a frisson, as if he were my guardian angel keeping tabs on me, followed by a pang of anxiety at the thought that I might never see him again.

Near the end of that year, I went with a friend to buy weed from an acquaintance of his, a fellow stoner who had picked up a little extra to hook up his buddies and make a few bucks in the process. We swung by an apartment building on Gayley, an ugly multiunit box. The shabby security vestibule opened on an elevator that stank of rancid hydraulic fluid. Upstairs, the hallway was anonymous and bland, but the apartment had a distinctive grotto-like atmosphere, the windows covered over with bedsheets and the walls festooned with posters, all of them for the same band, a band I had never heard of: Marillion. We stood awkwardly in the middle of the living room while a line of stoned residents deliquesced into the couch in front of us, eyes more wary than friendly. At the end of the couch, as stoned as the rest of them, sat my long-haired guardian angel. My friend got the pot, and, perhaps to make the visit seem less transactional, his friend made introductions around the room. I learned the name of the mystery man, a name not nearly as mysterious as he was: Jeff.

First quarter of sophomore year, there he was again, in Cinema and Social Change. Every Tuesday and Thursday, in Melnitz Hall, his myth disintegrated further, the slow grind of familiarity rendering him into just another undergrad, a fellow non-film major as clueless as I was about the movies we were discussing. This process struck me as curious. Over the years, it would spring to mind whenever I found myself having to deal with people whose fame summoned in me an irrational but persistent agitation.

The gate agent bent behind the counter to retrieve something from the printer. She handed Jeff his identification and boarding pass. He thanked her and turned to go. When he came past me, I said his name.

He looked at me quizzically.

"Yes?" he said.

"UCLA," I said.

His eyebrows went up behind those Lucite frames.

"Jesus," he said. "You look exactly the same. Plus twenty years or so, but you know what I mean."

I wondered if he was trying to place me. I started to say my name, but he beat me to it.

"That's me," I said.

"Names and faces," he said, tapping his temple. "It's a thing."

Oh God, I thought, he's become a salesman.

He put out his hand to shake.

"That film class," he said. "I remember. Only one I ever took."

"Same."

"Almost failed it. Couldn't stay awake in the dark. The whole thing felt like a dream."

"You didn't miss much," I said. I didn't mean it, but I was making conversation.

He smiled and took me in for a moment. "Hey, why don't you join me in the first-class lounge? I've got an extra pass."

"What about the flight?"

He pointed at the display above the gate. We'd been delayed.

I had already spent hours in the airport, my tickets having been purchased last minute and at the cheapest possible fare—a red-eye from LA, a layover at JFK, a flight to Frankfurt, a four-hour train ride to Berlin—and the idea of a first-class lounge was so appealing I could have hugged old Jeff right there and then.

I trailed him through the terminal, his soft-leather briefcase and fresh-looking roll-aboard making me wish I'd replaced my scruffy backpack with something more adult. The terminal wasn't packed, but it was crowded enough that we made better progress single file than two abreast. His hair was cropped cleanly in a line above his collar. Everything about him conveyed neatness and taste. In college I'd never seen him in nice clothes, only ripped-up jeans and weathered T-shirts worn inside-out to obscure whatever was written on them. Whether this was fashion or indigence was never clear to me.

The whole way from gate to lounge elevator, as I followed him and the rhythmic ticktock of his bag's wheels across the terminal's tiles, he didn't once look back to make sure I was following. I wondered if he was having second thoughts about inviting me into the land of the fancy people. I hoped I hadn't seemed too desperate when accepting his offer.

At the elevator, he was back to normal, or how he had been at the gate, delighted at the coincidence and looking forward to catching up, though as far as I knew we didn't have much to catch up on.

I presumed that he was one of those people who hated being

alone. Perhaps if I'd been paying closer attention, or if I'd known what was to come, I'd have detected a glimmer of desperation in his eyes. I don't know. Maybe it wasn't there, not yet.

We checked into the lounge at a marble counter, where an officious young man took my pass and waved us in, letting us know that they would be announcing when it was time for us to head down to the gate. Jeff found seats by the window, a low table between them, and gestured for me to sit, as if he were my host. The chair was real leather and the table real wood. He offered to grab a few beers. I hadn't had a drink in eight years but said that I'd be happy to watch him drink. He made for the food area, leaving his bags. Even in the airport's privileged inner sanctum, I couldn't look at the unattended bags without imagining they contained contraband, or a bomb. I put it out of my mind. My mantra for air travel has always been: Stop thinking. From the moment one enters the airport, one is subject to a host of procedures and mechanisms designed to get one from point A to point B. Stop thinking and be the cargo.

Jeff strolled up, two beers in hand. He put one in front of me, announcing that he'd found a nonalcoholic brew, and that he wasn't sure if I drank them, but he thought it might make things feel more ceremonial—that was the word he used—for us to catch up over a couple of beers, alcoholic or not, for old times' sake. We had never drunk together that I could remember, but I let it go. We clinked bottles and sipped, our eyes turning to the plane traffic outside.

"The miracle of travel," he said. "Fall asleep someplace, wake up halfway around the world."

"I can't sleep on planes," I said.

"I know a woman," he said, "friend of a friend, you could say, who is terrified of flying but has to travel to various places every year for family obligations. Only flies private, by the way, this is a very wealthy person. And here's what she does. An anesthesiologist comes to her house, knocks her out in her own bed, travels with her to the airport, to wherever she's going, unconscious, and when they arrive at the destination, she's loaded into whatever bed she's staying in, whether it's one of her other homes or a hotel, and he brings her back. She literally goes to sleep in one place and wakes up in another."

"Someone should do that for us in economy," I said. "You could fit a lot more people on every flight. Sardine style."

Jeff sipped his beer.

"You have business in Frankfurt?" he asked, his eyes passing over my scuffed sneakers.

"Berlin," I said. "My publisher is there."

I didn't mention that I was traveling on my own dime, hoping to capitalize on a German magazine's labeling me a "cult author." Or that I was also taking a much-needed break from family obligations, carving out a week from carpools and grocery shopping to live the life readers picture writers live full-time.

"I can't imagine writing a book," he said.

"Neither can I."

I'd said it before and meant it every time, but people always took it as an expression of false modesty.

Jeff laughed slightly. His demeanor changed, and I expected him to ask if he should have heard of any of my books. Instead, he asked if I'd ever gone under.

"I had my tonsils out in high school."

"Did you worry you wouldn't wake up?"

I shook my head. "Didn't cross my mind. Though were I to go under now, I wouldn't be so cavalier."

"You have kids."

"Two."

"Changes everything, doesn't it?"

He had undergone surgery recently, nothing serious, or not life-threatening at least, but he had ended up terrified that he wouldn't wake up again. It did happen to people. And though such accidents had become exceedingly rare, he couldn't help but imagine his going to sleep and never waking up, what it would do to his children—he had two as well—and to his wife. The whole episode had disturbed him greatly.

"Sleep is the cousin of death," I said.

Outside, a jumbo jet came in for a landing, too high and too fast and too far down the runway, at least to my eyes, and maybe to Jeff's too, since he watched it as well, but it came down fine, slowed dramatically, and made for the taxiway like any other plane. All the activity outside—the low vehicles buzzing around, the marshalers and wing walkers guiding planes with their orange batons, the food service trucks lifting and loading, the jetways extending, the segmented luggage carts rumbling across the tarmac—all of it vibrated under the gray sky like a Boschean tableau.

While I had been watching, he had been hunting down a thought.

"Coming out of surgery," he said, "waking up in the recovery room, foggy as hell, I didn't feel the sense of relief I had expected to feel—that only came later when I saw my family again. I felt like I'd lost a chunk of time. Like sleep, but when you sleep you wake up where you went down. I felt that things had happened to me without my knowledge, which they had, of course, and I was left with the uncanny sense that I wasn't the same person who had gone under. Time had passed, a part of my body was no longer in me, I had had a square shaved from my leg for some kind of circuit-completing electrode, but I was still I, obviously. Now, this may have been a side effect of the drugs, but I couldn't shake the feeling that I'd only just arrived in the world, as a replacement for the old me. It wore off, as I said, but it wasn't a pleasant state."

"Like a near-death experience?" I asked.

"Funny you should say that," Jeff said, as if he hadn't just nudged the conversation in that direction. "I ended up in close proximity to one once. Not long after college, in fact, a year or so later. I was, through no planning or forethought on my part, responsible for saving a man's life."

I wondered why he emphasized "no planning or forethought" when that would have been the default.

"What happened?" I asked.

"Let me grab a few more beers first."

"No, no," I said. "These are on me."

"They're free."

"Let me get them, then."

He settled into his chair.

I rose and made my way past a variety of travelers, from business types to trust fund hipsters, many of them speaking foreign languages. They weren't so different from their counterparts downstairs, other than not looking like they were undergoing an ordeal. I ordered beers from the dour bartender. It was not quite noon. When I returned to our table and handed Jeff a bottle, he raised it for another toast.

"Running into you was serendipitous," he said. "You were there at the beginning."

2

"The beginning?" I asked.

"The film class," he said, "with the Nigerian professor."

"Ethiopian," I said.

Jeff looked dubious. "You sure?"

"We watched a Nigerian film, but one hundred percent the prof was from Ethiopia."

Jeff was silent for a moment.

"All these years," he said, "I've been thinking he was Nigerian."

"Changes your story completely."

He caught my smile.

"Okay," he said, "we were in the film class. You, me, my girl-friend Genevieve, who went by G. You remember G?" he asked.

I didn't.

"She was unremarkable," he said. He leaned back like some-one who was used to being listened to. "Not that I knew it at the time. Tragically conventional. A film student, the most talented filmmaker in her class by a mile. Top-notch, professional-level work, or so it seemed to me then. But it wasn't just me. Her pro-fessors were always gushing over her stuff, talking about grad school, telling her she had a bright career ahead of her if she was willing to put in the work, and so on. Then, senior year, there's a thesis film awards ceremony, and the top prize goes to some-one else, a guy, which is bad enough, but a guy whose film was a complete mess."

"That sucks," I said.

"Yeah, I expected G to protest the decision, at least behind closed doors—she was a strong person, driven, but instead she told me that the judges confirmed what she had known all along, that while she might have been gifted in the craft, her work was bloodless. This was a gross distortion, as far as I was concerned.

Her work wasn't bloodless—people had been moved by it. But she wouldn't budge. Once she had decided on something, that was that. She was that kind of person.

"After graduation, she ended up at one of the talent agencies—she wanted to know the business from the inside. It was an insane job with insane hours, but she loved it. Meanwhile I picked up work with a startup, an internet-based city guide, like a curated yellow pages, this was back when the search engines had human editors indexing and categorizing stuff. The upshot of which was that my days were unstructured and full of roaming while she was tethered to desk and phone. It made me anxious, that imbalance, though I don't think I could have put it into words at the time, and so—it's amazing how these things cascade—drunk on champagne at her father's second wedding, I proposed to her. I don't think I wanted so much to be married as I was trying to wipe out the anxiety I was feeling about our inevitable drifting apart. I have to give her credit, she didn't say no. She laughed and kissed me. When we got back to Los Angeles, though, she'd already made up her mind. She had seen the future, and it didn't include our being together. As far as she was concerned, there was no point in prolonging things. Broke both our hearts. I thought we could choose not to be brokenhearted, by deciding to stay together, but like I said, she had a strong personality."

"Ouch," I said.

"She was right, of course."

"Still," I said.

"I loved her, by which I mean I loved the idea of her. It wasn't until a while after we had split up that I began to see how the real her, the actual her, had been obstructed by the *idea of her* I carried around in my head."

He swigged his beer.

"In the wake of the breakup I was miserable, no real money,

no close friends. I was living in a house in the canyons, house-sitting for an actor I knew. Actually, I was house-sitting for an actor who was house-sitting for an actor. I had nothing going on."

"Sounds familiar," I said.

"Jesus, that was a long time ago."

3

One morning, he said, he awoke to the sound of air whistling through G's nose, only to discover that the source of the sound had been his own nose, congested, and that he was alone.

Since they'd broken up, Jeff had found himself remembering and cherishing things he couldn't have imagined caring about when they were still together. Such was the case with the whistling sound G sometimes made when deeply asleep. The part of him that loved her most tenderly, like the love one might feel for a small, fragile animal, had been activated for him by memories of the nocturnal whistling, faint and rhythmic and above all suffused with a vulnerability she didn't display in waking life, perhaps because she herself was small, a few inches above five feet, barely a hundred pounds. When her breath coursed through the tiny gap in her sinuses or septum or nose itself, it sang a song of shields-down, of a kind of sweetness she rarely allowed him to see. The nose from which that song issued, a wonderfully convex-bridged, slightly out-of-proportion nose, balanced on either side by freckles on either cheek (only later did he realize that people must have treated her like a child), that nose became for him a special feature, which by interrupting her otherwise delicate beauty, enhanced it.

He thought about going back to bed. In that bed, the actor's bed, he and G had run through baby names, joke names, pure hubris, but acknowledged as such, which he thought might lend them a little protection. In that bed, in that house, they had played at adult life, pretending that they had furnished it themselves, that the art on the walls had been purchased on impossibly expensive trips to far-off destinations. The duck painting picked up on La Rambla in Barcelona, the kilim from a man with shaky hands in Istanbul. He would pretend not to know where the dishes had come from, and she would spin a tale of their origins. In creating a glamorous past they were also envisioning a glorious future. Now, though, everything vibrated with false provenance, the house echoed with associations, both fictional and real, the lightest and most playful now the most oppressive.

He needed out. He dressed, climbed into his old Volvo, and drove west toward Santa Monica.

The sun was not yet up. From atop the bluffs the beach was a dark gray strip, the ocean black. In the dark he walked across the pedestrian bridge over PCH, from one pool of light to the next. The beach lot was empty, nobody around other than a cyclist whizzing past, chasing an amber beam emanating from a box on his handlebars. The sky was a deep brown-black, low clouds reflecting the city's light back onto itself. A distant lump in the sand was either a nuzzling couple or a sleeping homeless person.

The immensity of the ocean was already having an effect on him, diminishing the size of his problems, connecting him to everything elemental and all-but-eternal.

He took off his shoes and socks, then stepped barefoot onto the cold sand, feeling a sense of liberation at his own insignificance, while also feeling—because he was alone, because it was dark, because the entire city lay behind him, asleep—a sense of himself as a sort of local god, surveying his domain under a cloak of invisibility and omnipotence, two sides of the same coin.

He sat at the water's edge, the dry sand just above the high-tide line, and the cold seeped through the seat of his pants. He could make out the horizon, splitting the view, the most distant visible thing on Earth. He fantasized about being dropped off out there, halfway to Japan, treading water, succumbing to exhaustion. He didn't know then that from his vantage the seemingly infinitely distant line was less than two nautical miles away. He was no better at estimating the dimensions of his heartbreak. With G, he'd felt like he was going somewhere, building a life, and now he felt like he'd been sent back to the starting line. As absurd as it would seem to him later, and actually impossible to re-create in his memory, to recapture the intensity of it, G's absence from his life felt unrelenting and ever present, the first thing he thought of upon waking and the last thing he thought of before sleep descended.

A glow simmered behind him, fiat lux, a slow reveal, coaxing sea and sky from the void. Another day begun. Pelicans skimmed the slick water. The hazy outline of a ship appeared in the channel. Nearby seagulls squabbled over a piece of cellophane. High-tide crests peaked but didn't break until they met the shore, ripples crossing the ocean from whatever storm had drummed them up, a rising of the waters, energy passed from one molecule to another like a baton in a relay, transmitted all this way only to fizzle out on the sand.

Just passing through, said a voice inside his head, source unknown, probably a bumper sticker. This happened sometimes—a voice or a song appeared in his thoughts, unbidden but germane to whatever was going on in the moment, as if he didn't have one mind but many and his consciousness worked more like an orchestra conductor than a generator of its own ideas.

Out of the corner of his eye he caught a dark form on the surface of the water. He was pretty sure it hadn't been there a moment before. A clump of kelp? No, a swimmer, making for the shore, an arm slapping the water, then drifting, as if scanning the bottom, like a snorkeler without a snorkel, but then, not. The swimmer undulated with the passing swell. The lack of muscle tension signaled to Jeff that something was wrong. He stood to watch, expecting the swimmer's arm to rise to slap the water again, or his head to turn for a breath, but nothing happened. He went to flag a lifeguard, but the towers were shuttered. Up and down the beach there was only a single woman jogging, too distant to take notice.

He hadn't yet faced a moment like this in his life, one in which he knew, with certainty, that the crisis at hand was his alone to handle. One during which he wished for the intercession of the god he didn't believe in, or anyone who might know what to do, or even someone as clueless and panicked as himself who could by their presence share the burden. It was one of those crucial moments, one which when reflected on wouldn't be laughed off but would send a chill up his spine, because even if he felt that he had no choice, that anyone would have done what he did in that situation, he would have to acknowledge that he was being tested, because in truth he could have given up, could have despaired, could have walked away, could have pretended he hadn't seen what he'd seen, could have subtracted himself from the scene, told himself that he wasn't even there, that he'd left a moment too early or arrived a moment too late, that the predicament had not in fact fallen in his lap but only grazed him as it passed undisturbed and unaddressed, left to unfold by itself, as nature might have intended.

I pointed out that one's interceding or not could equally represent fate, that letting nature take its course could include any number of interventions, since we ourselves were inseparable from nature.

He considered this for a moment, seemed about to reply, and sipped his beer instead.

4

The water was so cold, he continued, after he'd polished off the beer and fetched another, that it took his breath away. He felt like he was unable to get enough air into his lungs. Nevertheless, he made for the body, stomping through the shallows in his underwear and T-shirt, and then swimming, thinking that the man was probably okay, that he was being foolish, that the man would pop his head up at any moment and bring to an end what would forever become an embarrassing story about Jeff's tendency to jump to conclusions, to act before considering consequences. These thoughts alternated, round-robin, with others, equally powerful and clear, that this man was dead and had been dead a long time and was only drifting to shore. But hadn't he seen an arm slap the water?

The cold bit into his hands and feet, and though he swam with his head up, he tasted seawater with every stroke. When he reached the body he hesitated to touch it. What if it sprang to life and dragged him down with the last of its energy, as drowning people were said to do?

He took hold of a shoulder and tried to flip the man onto his back, but without being able to touch the bottom, he couldn't get the leverage he needed. He grabbed the man's hand and towed him the short distance to shore, swimming an awkward one-armed breast stroke, scanning the beach for anyone he could call on for help. At the inshore ditch he went underwater and shoved the body from below, using a ripple of swell to propel it onto the sand. It rolled, came to rest on its back, limbs folded awkwardly as if it had fallen from a height.

He stood before it. A middle-aged man in a slick swimmer's wetsuit, tinted goggles, bluish skin, purple lips. He had thought of him as both a he and an it, a man and a body, but now the form on the sand had resolved into a human being, a he, definitively. No sign of breathing, and he had no idea how to take a pulse. He didn't dare remove the goggles for fear of revealing eyes wide open but unseeing.

He dragged him away from the water's edge, wavelets erasing the track he left in the sand. The jogger was closer now but not yet upon them. The closest telephone was at the beach lot. If he had run back then to dial 911 would anyone have blamed him?

He had seen CPR on television but had no idea how it was really done. He put his hands on the man's chest, locked his elbows, and pumped. The sternum felt like a spring-loaded plate. Water leaked from the side of the man's slack mouth. He counted the compressions uselessly, not knowing when to stop. He knew what came next and didn't hesitate. The lips were cold, the stubble rough. He blew into the man's mouth and water sprayed onto his cheek. He had neglected to pinch the nose.

The chest rose and fell with his breath, but only as a bellows fills and empties. The skin looked no less blue. A feeling of disgust threatened to overtake him, spurred by the idea that he wouldn't be able to save this man, meaning he wasn't breathing air into a human being who needed help but into a corpse.

The jogger appeared, stopping in her tracks twenty feet away. He cried at her to get help and she ran toward the highway.

He returned to pumping the chest. Something cracked under the heel of his hand, and with each subsequent compression he could feel the break in the bone.

Salt water poured thick and foamy from the man's mouth. Nobody would have blamed Jeff for giving up. He wiped the foam aside with the back of his hand and breathed for the swimmer again, trying not to retch. Then to the sternum, the compressions, trying to put out of his mind the feeling of bone scraping against bone.

A seagull stood in the sand not five feet away, watching, its eye black like a wet seed.

Jeff tried to think of himself as a machine, doing the job of the man's heart and lungs, an incessant cycle of breaths and compressions. This went on and on. He wondered when would it be okay to stop.

But stopping would mean leaving the man for dead. He couldn't do that. It wasn't who he was. Someone else would have to come, someone who could take over, a professional, maybe, who could look at this body and determine that there was no saving him and bear the burden of giving up. When would that person arrive? Overcome with exhaustion but seeing no other choice, Jeff continued the compressions, the breaths.

The body convulsed. The swimmer gasped for air and coughed a cough unlike any Jeff had ever heard, sharp and wet at the same time. He rolled away from Jeff, vomited in the sand, moaned, tore off his goggles, vomited again.

Jeff sat paralyzed, exhausted and in awe, confused as to what to do next. He heard the blood coursing through his ears. His gut twisted. He started to shiver.

Spectators materialized. Had they been watching from a distance? One asked if the swimmer was okay. Jeff didn't answer. He wasn't even sure they were asking him.

A lifeguard truck rolled up, lights flashing. An old-timer emerged from the cab, red jacket, red shorts, ruddy face, silver mustache, moving with the equanimity of a lion on the veldt. He crouched by the swimmer, asked questions: What was his name? Did he know where he was? The day of the week? The mumbled responses were inaudible to Jeff. The lifeguard wrapped the swimmer in a gray wool blanket. Two medics in wraparound sunglasses came marching across the sand, each carrying an orange case, their ambulance idling in the beach lot behind them. Help had arrived and was continuing to arrive.

The swimmer tried to sit up, groaning in pain, but was kept supine by the medics, who affixed an oxygen mask to his face.

Jeff asked for a blanket, and it took a moment for the lifeguard to recognize that the long-haired young man before him, in T-shirt and boxers, had been involved and was soaked and hypothermic. He fetched another blanket from the truck and tossed it to Jeff. Jeff pulled it tight over his shoulders. The lifeguard turned his attention to Jeff, and Jeff stood to answer his questions. Dennis—per the name tag, though whether it was a first or last name was never revealed—asked him to describe what had happened. Jeff saw that Dennis's mustache wasn't entirely silver but had patches of yellow in it. As Jeff ran down everything that had occurred, he watched Dennis's eyes go from squinting to wide open, his crow's-feet stretching to reveal little folds of paler skin usually hidden from the sun. Dennis said that the swimmer had been very fortunate that Jeff had been on the beach. This could have been a very different call, he said, as if concerned mainly with the progress of his morning.

The swimmer clutched his chest and moaned again. Dennis went to the truck to pull out a wooden board with straps attached to it. He and the medics started securing the swimmer to it.

The swimmer turned his gaze to Jeff for the first time. With the oxygen mask on his face he was the inverse of the man Jeff had pulled from the water, nose and mouth now covered, eyes exposed, one lid slightly drooping, whether congenital or from the trauma it was impossible to say. His eyes were light, blue or green, and together with his furrowed brow, conveyed puzzlement. He raised his arm a few inches, as if he might point at Jeff or make some other gesture, but a medic guided it back down and strapped him in.

I saved your life, Jeff wanted to say. But it was for the swimmer to say, not him.

More people gathered to see what was going on, and in an effort to get closer, a few moved in front of Jeff. Dennis and the medics loaded the swimmer onto the back of the truck. With the tailgate down and a medic on either side, they rolled toward the beach lot.

The onlookers returned to whatever they'd been doing with their morning, and Jeff was left alone. He gathered his pants, his socks, his shoes—the trail of panic he'd left on his way into the water. He peeled off his soaked shirt and, under the blanket, his underwear. Then he pulled on his dry pants.

The ambulance left the beach lot, sirens howling, and the life-guard truck U-turned away from the lot. Jeff stood, expecting it to return to him, but after heading his way for a moment, it turned south toward the pier. Perhaps Dennis hadn't seen him standing there, or had been called away to handle another emergency.

Jeff collected his shoes, shirt, and underwear, then trudged across the sand to the spiral ramp that led to the pedestrian bridge. Joggers and walkers gave him wide berth. None would meet his eye. Wrapped in a rough wool blanket, barefoot, with disheveled long hair, shirtless, he must have looked like just another of the hard-luck cases wandering aimlessly around that so-called paradise.

5

"A hero," I said.

He looked out the window, then at his nails. A quiet "I wouldn't" escaped from his lips, and he seemed a different person from the one who had described the rescue in such vivid and energetic detail. I sensed that he wasn't sure how or even whether to proceed.

"You must have felt a sense of pride in what you'd done," I said.

He sipped his beer. "I was exhausted. I got back to the house and collapsed on the bed. Didn't get up until the afternoon. Only then did it occur to me to call somebody. My first thought was G, but we'd put a moratorium on communication after one too many late-night drunk dials. Dylan, the actor friend whose house-sitting gig I had taken over, was shooting in Vancouver. My other college buddies Emilio and Mark—remember them?"

I did not.

"They'd moved to the South Bay after graduation and I'd lost touch with them because of the G thing, classic case of guy meets girl, guy abandons friends. I knew I could call them, and that they'd let me right back in, but I knew also how they would react to my story—big congratulations and a round of drinks. You know, walk me up to a girl in the bar and tell her that I'd just saved a man's life."

"Not what you wanted," I said.

Jeff finished his beer, set the bottle down a bit too hard.

He shook his head.

"I didn't want to be celebrated, no."

"But you'd done something remarkable."

"That's how they would have seen it."

"And you?"

"I might as well have had a gun to my head. I'd acted on instinct, or at least on the fear of what would happen if I didn't act. I would never have chosen to find myself in that situation. In fact, I resented it. I didn't want those images in my head, the purple lips, cold, the broken ribs scraping, not to mention that I had no idea whether the guy had actually made it, I mean, after the ambulance took him away, he could have succumbed to whatever it was that had left him floating there in the first place."

"To be honest, if you'd called me, I probably would have tried to buy you a drink too."

"I get it. But that would have been like dropping a manhole cover on everything."

"You were traumatized."

He brought his hand to his chin and cast his eyes down. He may have been considering my words. After a moment, he sat up straight, his forearms resting on the arms of his chair as if he were readying himself for electrocution.

"In any case," he said, "I ended up not telling anyone."

"Then."

"Ever."

I wasn't sure I'd heard him right.

"Surely I'm not the first person you've told this to?"

He nodded.

"You've been hanging on to this story for going on two decades, and now you tell it to me? Me? Come on. You're pulling my leg."

He removed his glasses, rubbed his eyes, put his glasses back on.

"Wish I was," he said. "You appearing out of nowhere must have sparked some old circuitry up in here." He tapped his temple.

"Assuming you're being serious—"

"Oh yes."

"Why didn't you tell anyone? You couldn't have been that averse to someone calling you a hero."

"That wasn't it. It just— It became impossible."

"How's that?" I asked.

"I don't want to monopolize our conversation."

"Not at all."

"Besides," he said, "I don't know if I should get into it."

I sat back and waited for him to make up his mind.

6

The next day, he continued, clearing his throat, he called in sick. Whether it was the chill, or whatever had caused his stuffy nose in the first place, or a coincidence, he ended up developing a terrible cold and fever, at times slipping into a state of delirium, reliving the rescue in his dreams, haunted by the reflective goggles and purple lips.

After the fever and cold had passed, he returned to the beach, hoping to tamp down the images circling in his head. To go there and have nothing happen, he thought, might overwrite his memories.

He went early again, parked on the bluffs. It was warmer than it had been before, with a light offshore wind blowing. The ocean was an antique mirror under low clouds, the horizon razor sharp. There were bigger waves in the water, long smooth blue walls collapsing all at once, trapped air exploding out the back in plumes. It was a different ocean. A good sign, he thought. The ever-changing ocean wasn't going to repeat itself.

The moment he stepped onto the sand he felt that what he was doing would prove futile, even ridiculous, though there was nobody but himself to find it so. Nevertheless he made his way to the water's edge, inhaling deeply the seaweed-tinged air. He had been brought here before, by what he wasn't sure, and now he was asking the place itself to reveal to him at least a whisper of what it had all meant, why it had happened the way it did, even though he knew that no such revelation would be forthcoming.

He went down to where he'd dragged the man from the water, judging from the landmarks in the distance: the pier, the beach lot, the lifeguard tower. Any trace of activity had already been erased, even the deep tracks of the lifeguard's pickup had disappeared into the random scalloping of beach sand. If only he could so easily wipe the event from his memory, he thought, while also castigating himself for thinking so. He had saved a man's life—had done the ultimate good deed—shouldn't he want to remember it? But that was the distance between the thing itself and its definition: he couldn't reduce the former to the latter.

The scene revealed nothing of what had happened. The event lived on only in his mind, or his mind and the swimmer's, whoever and wherever he was. Jeff paced at the waterline, then made his way back across the sand to the beach lot, feeling unfulfilled and confused.

Crossing the pedestrian bridge, he watched the cars pass underneath. It was rush hour. From his vantage he looked down into their windshields, a parade of strangers. He was struck by their people-ness, by their unique individual existences, doled out into each car.

Their faces revealed nothing. As if they were posing for passport photos. Or sitting in front of computer screens. He thought of, then pushed from his mind, the swimmer's unconscious face. Would he have been released from the hospital already? Or would he still be there, intravenous antibiotics trickling into his veins, along with an opiate for the pain of the broken ribs, ribs broken by the hard heel of a helping hand?

He would still be in the hospital, yes, wife, or friend, or sibling by his side, swallowed up by the hospital bed, heart monitor beeping, skin flushed and pink, hair dry but messy, like a baby after a bath. But what about his state of mind? Was he in shock? At peace? How much of what had happened remained in his memory? Was there a gap? The smooth cold ocean, the gray dawn, the repetitive stroke, breathing and kicking and pulling in his regular rhythm, a phrase repeating in his head to keep everything synchronized, as to a beat; then as if waking from deep sleep, hard sand and dry air where water had been a moment before, muscles weak, rawness in his nose and throat, retching, searing pain in his chest. The red outline of a lifeguard asking questions.

What is your name? What day of the week is it? The brusque ministrations of the medics, the ride across the sand, another ride to the hospital . . . What about the way he tried to raise his arm while looking at Jeff? Did he remember that? What had he been trying to do? Signal? Beckon? Acknowledge? Thank? Even if everything that had happened at the beach was a blur, or a blank, Jeff had no doubt that somewhere in that man lingered a remnant of that canceled gesture.

7

The lifeguard's wool blanket remained in the bathroom for another week, its odor of wet wool, seawater, and mildew diffusing
throughout the house, though he was inured to it, spending most
of the time indoors, in a depressive funk he attributed in part
to the loss of G, watching any movie he could find without a romantic plot or subplot, eating his way through the canned food
in the actor's pantry. A half dozen soups, refried beans, lentils,
garbanzos, diced tomatoes . . .

At the end of the week he ordered pizza. The delivery guy
asked Jeff about the smell. He retrieved the blanket from the
corner of the bathroom and washed it in the machine on cold.
He set the dryer to delicate. When it was dry, he folded it neatly
in thirds and slid it into a paper grocery bag.

He parked the Volvo on the pier and made his way down to
the lifeguard headquarters, an industrial box tucked between the
pier and an exercise area on the beach. Behind the building was a
walled-off yard for equipment, where he thought he might enter,
but it was locked up. He found a door on the side of the building,
beige, with rust and paint bubbles at the edges. He knocked, but
got no answer. He tried the knob and found himself standing
in a nondescript hallway, fluorescent lights stuck to the ceiling.
Laughter filtered down from above, coming from the stairs to
the right. He made his way up quietly, listening to the lifeguards
talk. One was calling the other a racist, and the other said he
called them like he saw them, and there was more laughter, which
stopped abruptly when Jeff arrived at the top of the stairs. The
room had windows all across the front and part of the sides, with
a view of the beach to the south of the pier. Lifeguard Dennis sat
leaning back in a wheeled desk chair. Also seated in similar chairs
were a wiry tanned young man with a small judgy mouth—a pro-

totypical eighties movie jerk—and an older guard, not quite Dennis's age, balding and wearing a shit-eating grin. All three wore red jackets and red shorts.

Jeff apologized for interrupting, held up the grocery bag, said he just wanted to return the blanket he'd borrowed.

He hadn't come in with a plan, but he had hoped he might at least be able to ask a few questions of a receptionist, maybe get a name for the man he'd rescued. Confronted with these three men, bursting with convivial bravado, he lost his nerve. The jerk-looking lifeguard nodded at a countertop to suggest Jeff set the blanket there and leave them to continue their conversation.

Dennis asked him if he was the kid who had helped pull a swimmer out of the water recently. Jeff said he was and that he wasn't a kid. Dennis told the other lifeguards what had happened, and any sign of jesting or exclusion disappeared from their faces. Dennis asked Jeff if he understood what he'd done, how exceedingly rare it was that something like that happened, how decisive and ballsy he must have been to do what he did. The other lifeguards nodded in agreement. If it hadn't been for Jeff, Dennis said, as he had said on the beach, but this time with more feeling, the guy wouldn't have made it.

"He's okay?" Jeff asked.

"Last I heard, yeah," Dennis said, "though his ribs might be hurting a little."

"If they don't crack, they don't come back," said the balding lifeguard.

"Is that a thing?" the jerk asked.

"Should be."

Dennis offered to walk Jeff out. On the way down, Jeff asked how he could be sure the swimmer was actually okay.

"Wife sent a fruit basket," he said.

"Married, then," Jeff said.

"Happy to pass on your info to him."

Jeff hadn't thought of this possibility. He imagined Dennis

calling and telling the man that someone else had been involved in his rescue. What if the man didn't remember him? He imagined waiting for the man to contact him, not knowing whether he ever would.

"I don't know," Jeff said.

"Damn good fruit basket."

"I'm not sure," Jeff said.

Lifeguard Dennis gave him a probing look and asked him to follow. They went down the corridor away from the door he'd come in, to a windowless storage room. Dennis pulled open a file cabinet, riffled through papers, and pulled out an incident report. He handed it to Jeff.

"That's your guy there. I'll leave it up to you."

Francis Arsenault, with an address on Mandeville Canyon Road. Jeff committed it to memory and handed back the report.

Dennis put it back in the file cabinet, closed the drawer, and looked at him seriously.

"I never showed that to you," he said.

He escorted Jeff out of headquarters, through a garage and into the walled-off courtyard filled with pickup trucks, paddle boards, Jet Skis, and other equipment. They came to a human-size door cut into the large vehicle gate, and Dennis thanked him for returning the blanket.

"Nobody returns the blankets," Dennis said.

8

"I would have kept the blanket," I said.

Jeff smiled. "It was a pretext. Nevertheless, I appreciated what Dennis said. It reinforced my view of myself as a good person, someone who is conscientious, who returns things. I don't think I would have been able to put it into words at the time, but I saw myself as someone who didn't do bad things. I guess the rescue could be included in that, but it didn't feel like the same category, it didn't feel like a gold-star moment. It was more of an I-had-no-choice moment, as I said earlier. Gun to the head. I suppose that if I'd had a sense of myself as a bad person, a truly evil person, I could have walked away, or short of that, run to the phone in the beach lot knowing that it would be too little too late, that I had sealed a stranger's fate. But that wasn't who I was. I was a returner of blankets. I was the good person I thought I was. Don't forget that."

Why would I?

A server cleared our drinks and let us know that the buffet was being stocked with lunch items.

Jeff nodded and said thank you but scowled involuntarily at the interruption.

"I drove straight to Mandeville," he said. "I felt that by going directly there I was committing to decisive action. I told myself that I was giving Francis Arsenault, whoever he was, a chance to complete his gesture, to say his piece, to demonstrate whatever it was he was trying to communicate to me before the paramedics strapped down his arm and carried him away. And, of course, to confirm that he was actually okay."

Jeff raised his finger, made sure I was looking at him.

"I say 'told myself' because—and this became clearer to me later, I didn't know this back then, I wasn't wise to it—to put it bluntly, we never really know why we do what we do. The part of our brains tasked with generating reasons doesn't care about truth . . . only plausibility."

He was insistent on making this point, in making sure I'd heard it, and wouldn't continue until I acknowledged it.

"Mandeville," he said. "It was a construction site."

"A fake address?"

He shook his head. "I talked to one of the guys working there. He said that the family had moved into a rental while remodeling their home. Though *remodel* makes it sound minor. This was one of those teardown jobs where you keep up a chimney and a wall so you can tell the city you're not starting from scratch. They were going from a ranch-style home to a contemporary folly with lots of glass and angles."

"Did he know where to find Francis?" I asked.

"He was a laborer. Didn't even know Francis's name."

"It could have been anyone's house, then."

"Right. I looked around for a posted permit, but the one I could find had only the name of the builder. Then I heard a car honking."

"Was it him?"

Jeff shook his head. "Next-door neighbor. Pulling out. She was irked that, in my haste, I'd partially, like two percent, blocked her driveway. I apologized and asked her if it was indeed Francis Arsenault's house. She looked at me like I was an idiot and said, 'No, it's the pope's.' Took me a second to register her sarcasm and then she drove around my car exaggeratedly, which she could have done the whole time, without any exaggeration even, but apparently it was a matter of principle."

"Welcome to the neighborhood," I said.

"Exactly," Jeff said. He looked over his shoulder at the sneeze-guarded buffet. "Let's grab a bite before everyone else hops on it."

I hadn't wanted to interrupt his story, but since he'd interrupted it himself, I offered to do what a voice in my head had been telling me to do for a while, which was to check on the flight. Jeff said he'd be happy to grab me a plate.

At the counter I waited behind a swarthy man arguing that he'd been promised lounge access. He was being disabused of that notion by an officious shiny-faced blond woman. Sleek and vaguely Scandinavian, she fit right in with the lounge's international feel, as if she belonged permanently in the air above the North Atlantic. It was hard to imagine her returning to an apartment in Queens, or, in fact, returning anywhere. The man arguing with her, a rumple-suited sad sack of indeterminate accent and origin, asked to speak to a manager. She stepped around the back of a partition and returned a moment later with a tall distinguished-looking man, someone who in his uniform looked as though he might play the role of a pilot. He moved the disgruntled man down the counter so the woman could attend to me. I saw, by her name tag, that she was the director of operations; his name tag had no title. She was the senior employee, but she had decided not to pull rank on the customer. Instead, in a sort of hospitality jiujitsu, she'd simply deployed a man. And in fact, as I checked in with her about my flight, the employee was saying essentially the same thing that the woman had said to the customer, but the customer was taking it in as if for the first time.

Having witnessed this, I wanted to signal to her, Saskia was the name on her tag, that I found the dynamic regrettable and that while I was impressed with how diplomatically she'd handled it, a part of me wanted to dress down the other customer and let him know that she was the one with all the power, that she had actually held his fate in her hands, but the smile she presented me with betrayed no frustration, no sense of victory or defeat, no sign of the miniature drama I'd just witnessed, and, most significantly, no invitation to share in camaraderie. It was as if the entire past had been wiped away and this moment, her smile, and her chipper "How can I help you?" might as well have been the big bang. I pulled the boarding pass from my pocket and asked about the flight. She glanced at it, typed into her terminal, its keys going clackety-clack, and as she read the screen she pursed her lips at what could not have been good news.

"The delay is ongoing," she said, "but they could clear it at any time."

I asked if she knew the cause.

"Eyjafjallajökull," she said with perfect facility. "It is acting up again. They say it won't be as bad as April, but who can tell?"

I was still trying to untangle the first word.

"The volcano," she said.

Her eyes betrayed a glimmer of amusement, a perverse delight at the vicissitudes of travel, the things-which-cannot-be-changed, the fates assigned to us by the same gods who abandoned us long ago. It was the spark we see in the eyes of the patrolman shutting down the snowy pass, the local who tells you that you can't get there from here, the mechanic who informs you that you're not going anywhere today.

She said she would be sure to make an announcement when she heard anything else.

With that, our interaction was over. She reset herself for the person waiting behind me.

I returned to our seats to find a feast laid out across several small plates on the coffee table, a nonalcoholic beer by my chair. Jeff, clear cocktail in hand, gestured for me to sit. I felt yet again like the guest, being treated well by a generous host. I wondered if this was only friendliness, or a habit of his, or something he was doing by design. He said it was a good thing he'd hit the food early—they were already running low on the good stuff. He'd procured cheeses, crackers, olives, a ramekin of caviar or roe, a smaller ramekin of unspecified cream, a few finger sandwiches, and a cereal bowl of fruit salad.

"I can never control myself at a buffet," he said. "Doesn't help that I knew I was getting food for two."

I told him about the volcano.

"You'd think they could just fly over it," he said. "But no matter. Where was I? Leaving Mandeville Canyon."

I reached for a tiny cucumber-and-cream-cheese sandwich. I hadn't thought I was hungry, but once I took a bite, I discovered I was ravenous.

9

Jeff spread cream onto a water cracker, then scooped a dollop of roe on top. This consumed all of his attention, assembling a snack like he was going to present it to a panel of judges on a cooking show. Then, satisfied with how it looked, he popped the whole thing into his mouth and chewed, eyebrows up, looking at me.

"I got back to the actor's house," he said, once he'd swallowed his bite and washed it down with a sip of his cocktail, "and rummaged around for the white pages, remember those? No Francis Arsenault. Either he was unlisted—as somebody would be who could afford to build a giant house on Mandeville—or my phone book's coverage didn't extend to that corner of the city."

"If they'd tried to get the whole city into one book, it would have been the size of a small refrigerator."

"Right. But I had a trick up my sleeve. Remember the job I was working, the online city-guide thing? Well, this was in the days of dial-up, and my boss had given me a modem to work with, meaning I had access to the nascent World Wide Web, as they used to call it. So I did what any of us would do first today—"

"A web search."

"Right. I started with Yahoo, because they were rumored to be sniffing around our company for a possible purchase, so I felt a subtle allegiance to them. Turned out not to be true, by the way, no idea what became of the city search site. And Yahoo delivered. I discovered, without much trouble, a business called Francis Arsenault Fine Art on Camden Way in Beverly Hills."

"A gallery?"

Jeff laughed. "You've never heard of him, I assume, which is fine, but I'm telling you now that in those days he was as well-known as Arne Glimcher or Larry Gagosian."

"Okay, those sound familiar," I said.

"Household names . . . in the right households. I look back now, of course, and I find it amusing that I'd never heard of him, that I hadn't recognized his name as soon as I saw it on the life-guard's report. But that's the way it is, isn't it? We learn something new and we can't imagine never having known it. We're crossing the Rubicon every day, every minute. Can't go back. Can't return to a time when that name meant nothing to me. Not even in my imagination. Every bubble burst by the pinprick of reality."

He made a balloon-popping motion with the little roe spoon.

"I went the next afternoon," he said. "At first I couldn't figure out where it was. I had no idea what to expect. I figured an inti-mate space, dark woods, old paintings displayed in the windows, but it turned out to be this big white cube tucked between two office buildings, with no sign on it other than the address. Only after I'd parked the old Volvo in the structure across the street did I walk up to the humungous frosted-glass facade and see the sign. *FAFA Group Show.* It was visible through a gap in the frosting on the glass, a strip of transparency in a field of translucency. I remember thinking that it couldn't be good business—how was anybody supposed to know what this place was?

"The door—human-size and transparent—was cracked a tiny bit, just enough so I knew it was open. I stood on the sidewalk, imagining myself walking in. Who would I find? Francis? No, he wouldn't be in front. A receptionist. And then I'd ask for Francis, right? And he would emerge from wherever, stand in front of me, and . . . what? What could I possibly say to the man?"

"I saved your life?"

Jeff shook his head. "See, that was the problem. I didn't want it to seem like I had come to collect anything. Even if Francis de-cided to show his gratitude at that point, it wouldn't be any more meaningful than when you remind a child to say thank you."

"What's wrong with coming to collect something?" I asked.

"It didn't seem right. It didn't seem like what a good person would do, to put it clumsily. You don't save someone's life to collect a reward. I certainly didn't. I didn't even feel like I'd been given a choice. And so I didn't want it to seem as though that was what I was doing."

"Why track him down, then?"

"I was asking myself the same question, trust me. I'm still asking myself."

"Seeking closure?"

"What, here?"

"No, I mean why you sought him out. To put an endcap on your traumatic experience at the beach."

He considered this. "Yes, that would have made sense to me at the time."

"And now?"

He held his hand up. "Stick with me here."

"Fair enough. Did you go in?"

"I crossed the street. There was a coffee shop next to the parking structure, cute little place with a patio. I went in, asked the woman behind the counter if people ever came over from the gallery. She said they were in and out all the time. Needed pepping up, she said, surrounded by that boring art all day.

"I took my Americano to a two-top on the sidewalk and waited. Maybe, I thought, he would come out and cross the street. Didn't know what I would do next, but it seemed better than going in and asking for him. If he came to me, I mean, even serendipitously, that would be different. I remember sitting there, waiting, watching the afternoon's shadows make their way across the street. They reached the sidewalk opposite, but the gallery still blazed white in the sun. How did they keep that thing so clean? I wondered. Parked there, watching nobody go through that door. Again, how could a place like that stay in business, I thought, no foot traffic.

"Occasionally, I did see signs of movement. Just inside the door there was a gap in the partition, with what looked like a desk behind it. Whoever sat at that desk could, while minding the gallery behind the partition, also see and interact with people coming in from the sidewalk. Sometimes I saw that person, but no Francis. The light turned yellowish, and the shadows creeped up the facade. I drank another Americano. My thoughts were going in circles. At one point it occurred to me that if I had in fact come for a reward, I could do very well for myself. Between the Mandeville house and this gallery, Francis Arsenault was obviously a wealthy man. What if he were to pay off my credit card debt? I put it out of my head. That wasn't what this was about. Or if it was, it wasn't for me to decide. I could only put myself in Francis's path and see what happened from there."

"You thought he would recognize you."

"Why not? I wouldn't have to remind him or ask him or in any way prod him for his gratitude. At the very least I had to give him a chance to see me again.

"The shadows had swallowed the entire building when I noticed a figure behind the frosted glass, walking the length of the gallery in front of the partition. I could see that it was a man, but I couldn't see his face, obviously, just the outline of him. He walked slowly and deliberately, as if he had a stack of books on his head. When he reached the clear glass door, the outline resolved into someone specific."

10

Francis Arsenault looked different than he had on the beach, his hair combed neatly, small wire-rimmed glasses sitting low on his nose. Nevertheless, he had the same drooping eye, the same tenderloin physique, the same five-o'clock shadow, the same mouth into which Jeff had breathed new life.

Francis didn't push through the door. Instead, he turned and talked to someone through the gap in the partition. He looked toward the other end of the gallery, and a tall young woman in heels stomped across toward him, stepping past and opening the door, then handing him a small zippered portfolio case. Had he called her to bring him the case or to open the door for him, or both?

He started down the sidewalk slowly, walking with the same level gait Jeff had noted when watching his outline. Jeff watched his face for any sign of pain, but from across the street he couldn't tell. Was he still nursing his ribs? He would have been, yes. But he had come into work.

Jeff scurried down the sidewalk on his side of the street, toward Brighton Way, keeping an eye on Francis. It wasn't difficult to gain on him. He thought he might be able to make it across the street at the end of the block, so that he could place himself in front of Francis, walking toward him on the sidewalk, and create a chance encounter. But the signals were not in his favor, and there was enough traffic to make jaywalking risky. When the walk signal lit up, Jeff walked diagonally across the intersection as briskly as he could without breaking into a run. Francis had already passed, continuing down the street. Jeff followed, careful not to overtake him. Francis might be meeting someone for early drinks. A bar would be an excellent location for a chance encounter. Much better than running into each other on the sidewalk. But Francis walked into a shop, not a bar. Only as he stepped in front of it did Jeff see what it was—a tiny lingerie boutique with a French name. He did not follow Francis inside but tucked into the next shop down, a gift store full of fancy and preposterously priced knickknacks.

The shopkeeper, a sturdy woman with maroon lips and a platinum bob, asked if she could help him, and when he said he was just looking, she raised an eyebrow, or at least he thought she did. He pretended to browse the Chinese vases and crystal paperweights, but his eyes were on the sidewalk outside.

He stood where he would be able to see Francis exiting, expecting him to return to the gallery after running this errand. It wasn't yet the close of business hours, so that would make sense. The shopkeeper hovered a polite distance away. Jeff checked the price tag on a ceramic elephant. Eight thousand dollars. He didn't have that much money in the world.

The shopkeeper came over, having decided to give Jeff the benefit of the doubt, or wanting to keep a closer eye on him now that he was fingering price tags. She was dressed in what looked like black silk pajamas. She told him about the elephant's origins, how the workshop in which it was made only put out a limited number every year, how both Nancy Reagan and Michael Jackson had purchased them recently, though she wasn't sure whether it was for themselves or as gifts.

Jeff saw Francis step onto the sidewalk, paper shopping bag in hand. He didn't want to interrupt the shopkeeper, but it was time to resume his pursuit. He made up an excuse, that his mother had been looking for an elephant and that he would be sure to send her in. By the time he stepped outside, Francis was already a hundred feet down the sidewalk, moving smoothly, purposefully, in the same direction he'd been walking before, away from the gallery.

Where was he going? Perhaps he had a parking spot under one of the buildings down the block. Jeff didn't think it was likely he was going to go to a bar with whatever he'd purchased at the lingerie shop.

Francis stopped at the crosswalk at Wilshire Boulevard, waiting for the walk signal. Was it possible he lived down here, in the residential area below Wilshire? Made sense, to rent a place near the gallery while the house was being redone. He might have been bringing home a little gift for his wife.

Jeff caught up. He stood not quite next to Francis. He easily could have tapped him on the shoulder. Aside from a woman standing several feet away, they were the only ones waiting for the signal. He hadn't realized how small Francis was, a head shorter than himself, almost. He stood in Francis's peripheral vision, he knew, because Francis looked briefly to the left, to assess whether Jeff was friend or foe. The glance wasn't nearly long enough for a positive identification, only a ruling-out. In Francis's world, someone who looked like Jeff—long hair, jeans, T-shirt—was background, atmosphere, as they said in the film business.

There was a box in the shopping bag, elegantly gift-wrapped.

They crossed Wilshire to the sounds of honking and revving from the congealing traffic. Outside the cocoon of the shopping district they'd just left, the winds blew wilder and the interactions were more anonymous. Jeff walked slowly but had to stop and pretend to look in the windows to avoid overtaking Francis. Every once in a while, he heard a hiss escape from Francis's lips, accompanied by a shift in his gait. The ribs. Jeff felt like apologizing then and there for what he'd done to this poor man's ability to move around without pain. Apologizing! He caught himself. The man wouldn't have been able to move at all if it weren't for him . . . he would have been six feet underground.

They came to a large building with striped awnings over its windows facing the street. Miniature manicured hedges in front. Stone columns, carvings up the walls. A giant American flag hanging from a pole at an angle, flanked by flags of other nations. A massive black Mercedes parked at the curb. It was far nicer than any hotel he'd ever been in, yet he felt he had seen it before. It had been in a movie probably, he couldn't remember which.

The doorman opened the door and welcomed Francis inside. Jeff thought he might have to sneak in after him, but the doorman, to his surprise, gave him an equally warm reception.

Half the lobby was taken up with a restaurant, and because he had already pictured Francis heading to a bar, Jeff expected to see him check in with the hostess. But Francis had lined up at the registration desk.

Jeff made a circuit of the lobby, checking his watch periodically as if he were waiting to meet someone. He tried to act casual, but he felt completely out of place in what seemed to him the acme of wealth and luxury. (Looking back, he found this amusing. He would never stay there nowadays and would never recommend it to clients. Faded glory, corporate ownership, cookie-cutter rooms. It was for tourists, boosted by its appearance in *Pretty Woman*— that was where he'd seen it.)

He found a bench between the elevators and sat to observe Francis standing in line behind another guest. Francis didn't look around, didn't seem to take in anything other than what was happening at the registration desk, where two different parties were checking in. He radiated the impatience of someone in line at the grocery store, watching the customer at the register pull out a checkbook, or worse, dig around in their wallet for exact change.

Once at the desk, Francis identified himself and was immediately handed a key. No driver's license, no credit card, no signature. He made for the elevators, walking directly toward Jeff. Jeff looked at his watch again, this time for Francis's benefit, though he wasn't sure Francis noticed. Francis seemed preoccupied. He pushed the UP button several times, stepped back. Jeff sat facing him, directly in front of him but on a different plane. Francis's eyes were on the indicators above the elevator doors.

Jeff was close enough to see Francis's chest move with every breath. He examined Francis's clothing up close now. It was obvious that what he was wearing was high quality, though it wasn't flashy in any way. Same for his watch. Jeff knew nothing about watches, but Francis's exuded understated elegance.

He was going up to a room, his room, a room he had stayed in before perhaps. Or a room he was staying in while his house was being remodeled. But that would have been prohibitively expensive. And there was the matter of the lingerie. A gift, judging from the careful wrapping.

Francis stood stiffly, as if stillness would render him invisible. He kept his eyes locked on the display, watching the floors count down. But why should he worry about being observed? Was Jeff's presence making him anxious?

Jeff realized it then. It was right in front of him. Francis had sought out the privacy and anonymity of a hotel room in an establishment where he knew he could rely on the discretion of the staff. He was having an affair.

The bell dinged, and the elevator doors opened. Francis glanced at the long-haired young man sitting on the bench. Jeff, of course, was looking at him already. Their eyes met. What did Jeff see in those eyes? Nothing he could read. Eyes as cold as the seagull's on the beach. Then Francis disappeared into the elevator.

Could he have chosen a worse possible moment to reveal himself? He had been so occupied staying hot on Francis's heels that he hadn't thought of anything else until the crucial moment.

He comforted himself with the knowledge that Francis was alive, definitively alive. He could rest easy knowing that he'd been successful. What did it matter whether Francis recognized him as long as he knew he'd actually saved the man's life? He didn't need acknowledgment. He'd avoided it. He'd done what any person would do—any good person—without an expectation of reward. It had worked, he had checked in on him—this was, he told himself, the reason he'd tracked Francis down—and now he could move on with his life and Francis could move on with his. The matter was settled.

Jeff watched people move through the lobby. It was early evening, the hour for end-of-day drinks, and patrons were coming in consistently to check in with the hostess. A few tourists, but mostly people dressed like they'd been sitting at desks all day. Occasionally, someone, or a couple, or a group of people, walked to the elevators and stood in front of him waiting for the doors to open. Other than a glance here and there, none of them acknowledged him.

Of the people who went up the elevators, several were single women. Might one be meeting Francis? Was it the brunette, in her midforties, dressed for a garden party? The woman of uncertain age, blond and severe? The twentysomething in a beige sweater dress, boots, and bright red lipstick? Then again, whoever Francis was meeting could have been waiting in the room already.

Jeff had been so close to Francis, inches away, yet they might as well have been on different continents. Francis had looked at him. A Francis anxious about an assignation. Had Jeff's face set off in Francis any twinge of familiarity? Was Francis right now upstairs wondering who that shabbily dressed kid was? If the tables had been turned, Jeff would have recognized the man who had saved his life. He would have scoured the earth to find that person. The way Francis had looked at him on the beach, the gesture he had made, interrupted by the paramedic . . . surely somewhere in that muscular skull, in a specific pattern of neuronal energy, lay an image, an imprint, of Jeff's face.

11

"You think so?"

"He raised his arm, he looked into my eyes. He had to have been laying down memories. My face must have gone in there somewhere, right?"

"I'm no neuroscientist."

"Me either, obviously. But I've thought about this. You've had the experience of remembering something you didn't think you remembered?"

"Sure."

"It's a labyrinth in here." He tapped his head. "And somewhere in Francis's labyrinth lay an image of me, I'm certain of it. Whether he was ever able to access it, I don't know."

"But he was okay, alive, healthy even."

"Sure."

"Your questions were answered, yes?"

He went to scoop more roe, but it was gone. He settled on a carrot stick. A busser came by and cleared our plates.

"Here's what happened," he said. "I got back to my car to head home, pulled into molasses-thick traffic on Sunset, and tried to tell myself it was over, properly over."

"Seems like it should have been, yes."

"But I felt like ramming the red brake lights of the car in front of me. Who was this guy, this Francis Arsenault, to not recognize what I'd done for him? I had given him new life."

"You were angry with him?"

"He was dead on that beach. Dead dead." Jeff paused to make sure I had absorbed his words.

"He was lucky you were there," I said.

"Right!" He raised his voice. "What if I hadn't been?"

"But you were."

He took a breath and looked out the window, collecting his thoughts.

"I told myself that he hadn't been given a proper chance to recognize me. Why should he have pulled from that soggy corner of his brain an image of my face? And match it with dry-haired me, in a hotel, far from the beach? I mean, with enough time, with the right cues, maybe, but the truth was I hadn't given him a chance."

"Maybe it was for the best," I said, "considering the circumstances."

"Yes, that's what I told myself."

"So you were done. Or did you orchestrate another encounter? Wet your hair first?"

"Funny you should mention the hair. No. I cut it off."

"What?"

"Saw a barbershop while driving the next day. Stopped in and told the guy to take it all off. Ended up with a George Clooney à la *ER*. Short-banged Caesar."

"On a whim?"

"I was going for a fresh start. Shedding the old mane felt like a fitting close to the G chapter of my life. I'm still a believer in a good shave and a haircut. That one was dramatic. All of my brokenhearted memories dropped away with the hair. More or less, anyway. I can still picture the barber sweeping it up."

"Unlikely Francis would recognize you after that."

He put up a finger. "I changed my mind. After I'd gotten over my anger or whatever it was, my indignation, I decided that I didn't necessarily want to be recognized. Something else had come to the forefront of my thinking. Recognition versus lack of recognition—that was all about myself. The real matter was: Who was this man whose life I'd saved?"

12

The question, he continued, once it took root, invigorated him. So did the haircut. He cleaned the house, shopped for proper groceries, and caught up on his work, maintenance of the city-guide website. Scrolling through the site's archive of user search queries was his favorite part of the job, and it reminded him of a valuable lesson. There is no more powerful skill for success in any field than knowing how to ask the right questions. A painter, for example, might be working on a body of work, asking, "Is it beautiful? Is it beautiful?" and that might be, unbeknownst to him, the wrong question. He might go completely astray in search of a quality that has nothing at all to do with where the work should be going.

The question occupying Jeff's mind, the one he'd come up with while watching his hair fall to the floor of the barbershop, or before, was large, was open, was broad. He decided to pursue answers the old-fashioned way, returning to his alma mater—*our* alma mater—to see if anything turned up in the electronic, paper, microfilm, or microfiche records of the University Research Library.

He found: A wedding announcement in the *New York Times*; several quotations in the same, about record sales at auction houses (the prices were staggering to Jeff); an interview in an alumni magazine about how he got started in his career; a *Los Angeles Times* magazine profile; several listings in various *Who's Who* volumes; court records—civil lawsuits; and an interview in a financial magazine about buying so-called blue-chip art as a hedge against stock market corrections. Francis was also mentioned in a number of magazine profiles of artists, usually in the form of a promotional pull quote.

Jeff copied and printed out everything he could find about Francis Arsenault, then went home, brewed a cup of coffee, and made his way through the documents.

13

First of all, Jeff discovered, his name wasn't Francis Arsenault. He was born Frank Busse, in Columbus, Ohio, in 1950, and was raised in unique circumstances. His father, Klaus, had been a labor lawyer and activist, and the family had moved wherever the work took him. They'd ended up in Columbus only because Klaus was there trying to push Robert Taft out of office in the senate elections that year.

Old Klaus refused to hold himself above the workers he represented, so despite having means, the Busse family always lived in working-class surroundings. Frank went to school with the children of the workers. His father believed that everyone should be treated equally. Frank's classmates didn't share the same belief. It didn't matter that his father was on their fathers' side. He had to fight them every day. Per several interviews, this "colorful upbringing" rendered him impervious to intimidation.

His grandfather, Alois Busse, whose industrialist successes Klaus's life was dedicated to combatting, passed away when Frank was twenty, leaving the bulk of his estate to his third wife, a Floridian ballroom dancer thirty years his junior. However, wanting to make up for the life his son had imposed on his grandson, Alois left his entire art collection to young Frank. A dozen modern European paintings, including a Picasso, a Braque, and a bunch of Germans Frank had never heard of. A small Henry Moore sculpture, and a Calder wire portrait supposedly depicting Alois himself. This work he remembered from one of his few visits to the old man's New York apartment. Lit from below, it cast an eerie shadow on the wall behind it, of a grotesque face. "The real Alois," his father had told him.

Whether the bequest was meant to encourage the young man's artistic aspirations or nudge him toward the world of commerce was unclear, but it had the latter effect. Frank first tried on the name Francis, coupled with his mother's maiden name, Arsenault, when selling off a group of German expressionist paintings. The idea was to disguise his association with old Alois, so that Francis might seem like a legitimate dealer, rather than a rich kid unloading family heirlooms.

He tried to walk straight into the art gallery scene in New York in the 1970s and found it insular, closed off, peppered with a limited number of top collectors over whom all the dealers sparred. He managed to get a job at Marian Goodman's Multiples, Inc., for a while, inspiring him to make two bold moves that would define the early part of his career. First, he would specialize in prints. Second, he would go to California. He knew that there were collectors in Los Angeles—he saw them or their representatives at the auctions and openings in New York—and he understood that below that level of collector was a massive underserved population of aspirants. People who couldn't afford a blue-chip painting but wanted to signal to their acquaintances—in a city where people routinely walked their guests around their homes to show off the decor—that they were au courant and connected to cultural products from beyond the world of Hollywood. They weren't the type to drop money on unknown and emerging artists. They wanted art that people would recognize.

He arrived in Los Angeles and discovered that others had already paved the way. He worked as an assistant at Gemini GEL in the period after Ken Tyler left, and though he didn't stay long, describing himself as "ultimately unemployable," he emerged with a Rolodex of artists, collectors, and other gallerists. He'd always been cagey about the next steps, skipping ahead to renting a space in Venice, with the obligatory "It wasn't as nice as it is today" comment, and hanging the FAFA shingle, under which he sold prints and multiples at first, then, once he'd established himself, dipping his toe into showing original work.

He married Alison Collins Baker, one of his artists, a few years later.

14

When asked the secret of his early success—a question that came up in several profiles—Francis always gave the same answers: "I didn't know enough to know what I didn't know." Or: "I discovered that I was good at throwing parties."

When he emerged from his chrysalis in Los Angeles, no longer Frank Busse but Francis Arsenault, art dealer, he discovered that people actually wanted to be close to him, wanted to know him. To collectors, he played up being the grandson of Alois, carrying on a family tradition of supporting the art scene. To artists, he was the lefty son of Klaus, a man who lived by his values, who knew hardship. To himself he was Francis Arsenault, his own invention, ex nihilo.

And Francis Arsenault had an eye. It came up in every interview, profile, and article. The eye.

"You were nothing if you didn't have an eye."

"Even those who manage to anticipate every trend are going to get tripped up somewhere without a good eye."

"When the bottom falls out—and the bottom always falls out—the good stuff holds value while the lesser work plunges. To know the difference takes a good eye."

But the eye didn't pay the assistants, the rent, the utilities. About the business end of the art world, Francis spoke as blandly and authoritatively as possible. The closer the conversation hewed to money, the more oracular he became.

Only one article talked about it in concrete terms. It focused on rumors of Francis's inflating a seller's price without telling the seller. Allegedly, he'd told the collector he could get $1.2 million for their picture, then turned around and offered it to another for $1.5 million, taking both his regular commission and the clandestine markup.

Among other nasty quotes in the article was this one from an "anonymous art-world insider": "The only reason Francis is in this business is because it's the most easily manipulated market in the world, and he's a master manipulator."

15

Every time Jeff read the word *eye*, he thought of Francis's drooping eye, the eyelid, to be specific, on the right side. Looking at the photograph accompanying one of the articles about Francis, he saw it there, not hanging low enough to obscure his vision but distinctly lower than the left eyelid, a sleepy look that conveyed both seduction and skepticism. Jeff spent time looking over the photos of Francis, or at the smudged black-and-white copies he had brought home from the library, trying to see in them not only the highly successful art dealer but also the boy who had grown up an outcast, the young man who had been rebuffed by the New York art establishment. He looked, too, at the photo accompanying the wedding announcement. Alison Collins Baker, of Greenwich, CT, was a beauty whose perfectly symmetrical face stood in stark contrast to Francis's. If Jeff were married to that woman, he thought, he certainly wouldn't be risking everything to meet up with other women in fancy hotels.

The articles and photographs had filled in a lot of information, but Jeff found himself feeling a frustration similar to what he felt when following Francis from his gallery, that the surface of the man occluded rather than illuminated his essence.

16

"I could have read a thousand pages of that stuff and he would have remained opaque," Jeff said.

"You didn't get a sense of the arc of his life?"

"Sure, but biography creates that. The arc doesn't exist otherwise. It's an illusion. It's a story about a shark compared to actually seeing a shark. There is no substitute for meeting someone in the flesh. In determining who they really are, I mean."

"You mean like getting a vibe?"

"In a manner of speaking," he said, tilting his head as if to say I hadn't quite hit the target. "It's not as binary as whether they're trustworthy or not. That's what I think of when I think of a vibe. Certain animal skills. What I'm talking about is far more subtle. Whenever two people interact, in person I mean, there's an exchange of energy. Or energies. An overlap. This phenomenon is so complex, it exceeds our ability to perceive it. We don't have the bandwidth."

I must have made a face because he sipped his drink, mainly ice at this point, and said, "You see where I'm going with this?"

"Go on."

"I needed access."

I looked out the window at the low-hanging gray skies, the passing jets, and luggage carts.

"You could have walked away," I said.

He frowned.

"It seems like that now, sure, almost twenty years on. But I wasn't who I am today."

"That's easy to say."

"Are you the same person you were then?" he asked.

"For the most part, yes."

"You stand by every decision you made in those days?"

"Fair enough."

"You have to recognize that this was a major event in an otherwise uneventful life. Nothing I'd done had ever resulted in such profound consequences. Just think, if I had somehow not saved Francis's life, if instead he'd died on that beach, everything that came after would not have happened like it did."

"To be fair, that could be said for many things. A butterfly flaps its wings . . ."

He put up his hand. "Some events have more impact than others. And the cascade of consequences spreads out over everything. That rendezvous in the hotel? Wouldn't have happened. The next gallery show? Same. Everything I'd read up on from UCLA, that would have been the end. A few obituaries would get tacked on, no more.

"But thanks to me, thanks to my intervention, Francis continued along his timeline."

"As if nothing had happened."

"Well, the episode left its mark on him too."

"How so?"

"I'll get to that. As for my state of mind, it was impossible for me to look at anything Francis-related and not feel that I was at least partially responsible for it."

"Like God in plain clothes," I said, quoting a book I'd read two decades before.

He leaned closer. "It started to sink in that I'd accomplished something. But what, exactly, remained to be seen."

"By you."

"By me."

"More like a spy than a god, then."

He shook his head. "A spy reserves judgment."

17

Jeff visited the coffee shop regularly, learned the name of the frizzy-haired woman behind the counter ("Molly—amazing what the mind retains"), and spent inordinate amounts of time watching the gallery across the street. It wasn't hard to imagine an alternate version of the gallery, one with a CLOSED FOR BUSINESS sign out front, or some such indicator that the man for whom the gallery was named had perished in an unfortunate swimming accident. He did this, now and then, imagined the alternate universe, to remind himself that he was the one responsible for the ongoingness of the one in which he and Francis and the rest of us lived. He was trying to gather the courage to cross the street and go in. He hadn't seen Francis since the day he'd followed him to the hotel. With each passing day he came closer to taking the plunge. What was stopping him? He wasn't sure. Fear of discovery? Of recognition? Perhaps it was wisdom. Perhaps he should have walked away, and a voice inside him was telling him to do so.

He didn't listen, of course.

Still he did not cross the street.

One day he was just about to leave the café when he spotted a FAFA assistant storming out of the gallery. Behind her the glass door clanged against its stopper so hard he was surprised it didn't shatter. She crossed the street on shaky heels, cheeks red and eyes brimming with tears. He'd seen her before, fetching coffees for the staff. This time she didn't walk into the coffee shop but went straight for the adjacent parking garage, mumbling a string of frustrated expletives. Two minutes later, she squealed away in a little silver Mercedes.

The next morning, Jeff came in, ordered his customary drink, opened his laptop, and looked across the street as usual. Tucked in the lower left corner of the massive windowed front of the gallery, pressed up against the frosted glass so as to be legible from outside, was a letter-size sheet of paper, on which someone had laser-printed the words *assistant needed apply within*.

18

"You didn't," I said.

He removed his glasses, held them up to the light to examine the lenses, pulled a shirttail to wipe them clean, and put them back on. He was stalling for some reason, or trying to milk a dramatic pause. He cleared his throat.

"Would that have been crossing a line?" he asked.

I said I didn't know.

"It would have been a different life—the last twenty years, I mean—if I hadn't."

19

Jeff stood before the partition that ran across the front of the gallery, peering into the small opening near the entrance. He saw a man—not Francis—on the telephone. He paused, wondering whether he should check in before proceeding, but the man was wrapped up in his call and paid him no mind. Jeff walked the length of the partition and stepped around it into the main gallery, an expansive bright white cube with ceilings that must have been twenty-four feet high. He could hear his own footsteps echoing on the concrete floor, as well as one half of the man's telephone conversation. The gallery was devoid of any other people. Jeff heard the man say *Francis* into the phone, and he felt a tightening in the pit of his stomach.

"Francis is going to need the pieces here before he's back from Kassel," the man said. "Or there's no show."

Francis was out of town, a relief. Jeff would have a moment to find his footing.

The man, curly-haired and olive-skinned, in his early thirties, sat behind a small desk-cum-counter on which a pile of brochures was stacked next to a business card holder. To the right, a series of stairs, marked PRIVATE, led up to what must have been offices. Jeff was surprised to see so few people. Whenever he sat across the street, watching people go in and out, he pictured the gallery as a beehive of activity.

He stepped into the back gallery, feeling as if he were trespassing. It was as free from human presence as the front room and as suffused with natural light. At this point he allowed himself to absorb what hung on the wall. Until that moment the art had been only rectangles in his peripheral vision, objects that were where they were supposed to be. He'd have noticed only if they'd been absent. The back room was hung with large-scale paintings of energetic colorful strokes in a variety of styles. One painting depicted a house-like structure, but the others were entirely abstract. He thought what many had thought before and what many would think again: a child could have made these.

He examined the wall labels, surprised that so many of the works lacked titles. None of the artists' names meant anything to him. He was relieved to see no prices listed. He concluded from this that FAFA sometimes functioned as a museum or nonprofit exhibition space. This made him more charitable toward the work: despite it not being to his taste, he allowed that it might have emerged from a sincere desire on the part of the artists to express themselves, and who was he to argue with that, as long as they weren't ripping people off.

The man at the desk finished his phone call, which took a surprising turn at the end, an "Okay, love you" out of nowhere. Jeff returned to the main gallery, making for the desk. The man behind it was scribbling in a notebook. After a moment of Jeff standing there, he looked up.

"I'm here about the job," Jeff said.

The man looked him up and down and smiled as if relieved to see him.

20

His name was Marcus, and, he said, he was eager to be off the floor and upstairs, where he had unimaginable amounts of work to do. The job was simple, if you were cool babysitting artwork, shooing tourists, and getting yelled at.

He raised his finger. "All while looking good," he added. "You can't look sloppy."

Then, realizing he'd jumped forward a few steps, he asked Jeff about his experience.

Jeff said that he'd just graduated from UCLA. Marcus mentioned the excellent art history department, and in his overall nervousness at the situation, Jeff nodded without saying anything else. Marcus took this as Jeff's having majored in it, despite his never having taken a single class in the subject, knowing that as soon as the lights went down and the slides came out, he would have been fast asleep.

Marcus showed him a single page in a glassine sleeve, told him he would be the keeper of the price sheet. Several of the titles had red dots next to them, Jeff didn't know why. He was still trying to absorb the fact that the works were, indeed, for sale, and that the numbers were the prices. There were no dollar signs next to them, though they must have been in dollars, but the figures were far too large to be actual prices for actual works hanging on the gallery's walls. These figures were ludicrous, money a sensible person might use to buy a house.

He didn't ask any questions, for fear of appearing a rube, and acted as if everything was just as he'd expected.

Marcus explained that Jeff was to let people see the price list if they asked but not let them take it away from the desk. If they looked like they were taking notes, he should alert Marcus by pinging his extension. In fact, if he had any questions at all, he should always ping Marcus. Answer the phones, but don't take any questions. Take messages. If they ask for Francis, ping Marcus. If they ask for *anyone*, ping Marcus.

He asked Jeff if he was available to start right away. Jeff said he was.

"Thank God," Marcus said. "We'll deal with paperwork later, but as of this moment, you're hired."

"I do have a few questions," Jeff said.

"Later. For now, sit there, look pretty. Shouldn't be hard for you." He winked. "Look like someone who would be sitting behind the desk at an art gallery. And don't let anyone walk out with any paintings."

What happened that first day? Not much. Relieved of his fear that Francis would show up, Jeff replaced it with a fear that he would be called upon to sell the art. But nobody who came in seemed interested in buying it. They walked through the gallery, pointing at work, and then, usually, left with a quiet thank-you. Jeff tried to make himself look official by scribbling on papers, as he had seen Marcus doing. The job, that day at least, consisted of exactly what Marcus had said: sit there, look pretty. And endure the silence, or, if there were visitors, echoing footfalls and hushed comments. Only one person asked for the price list that first day, an older woman with a pixie haircut and a red pair of readers sitting low on her nose.

"Oh," she said. "I see it's sold. Shame."

That was when he figured out that the red dots meant the work had been sold.

"Do you know if it went for this?" she asked.

He stared at her blankly, then went to ping Marcus's extension.

"No, no," she said. "Don't bother. *They're* not going to tell me."

When the gallery was empty, he found himself looking at the stairway to his left, the sign marked PRIVATE. Marcus was up there, somewhere. Jeff could hear him on the phone. And a woman too.

He wondered what could have possibly happened with his predecessor to make her cross the street in tears. Had it been him they would have been tears of boredom. He remembered what his mother had told him when he was a child: "Waiting is doing what you don't want until you get to do what you want." He would bide his time in the new sinecure, waiting for Francis.

Day after day, new red dots appeared on the price sheet. Selling was happening, just not when he was there, not in front of him. This despite the fact that he had to sit with the works all day. It lent a sense of unreality to his days.

Marcus, of ambiguous ethnicity and sexuality, driven by some undisclosed privation in his youth, came at Jeff with a flurry of code-switching, trying to get a bead on the new kid's coordinates. Jeff was called "dawg," "bro," "dude," and "Holmes," and in each instance Marcus didn't sound like an old person trying on slang. Each argot, from surfer to hustler, sounded as genuine as the last. He seemed, at least in those first days, like a chameleon, a connoisseur and a merchant, aesthete and peddler. He was always off to meet a "friend," which could have meant any of a million different things.

Cooler was his cohort Andrea. In her forties, focused and unattached, she was impeccably put together. Rose lip liner, tight bun. At first Jeff thought she was excited only by gossip and money. Then, one afternoon, he heard her going on and on about scuba diving. This was what lay at the center of her life. Everything she did at FAFA was in service of her next trip, her next journey under the surface of the sea, to Belize, or Mexico, or the South Pacific, to swim among fish and coral and seaweed. Jeff found her more easy to understand when he realized that her real life was down there, underwater, absorbed in quiet isolation, and that the world of the gallery—in fact all the world on land—was subordinate to it.

It was impossible to tell what either Marcus or Andrea thought about the artists, or art in general.

Rafe, in shipping, hated Jeff right away, seemingly for no reason. And Naomi, a fellow assistant, had asked him what the hell he was doing there, if he wasn't an artist and didn't want to be a dealer. He had no answer for her. There were others, too, and though he didn't meet them early on, he was aware that news of his arrival had rippled through the small circle of FAFA employees, and that he was initially perceived as a cipher.

"There's power in being a cipher," Jeff said. "Especially in a business that trades on information. Not that I had any idea."

He sat back with his hands intertwined behind his head and his legs crossed at the ankles.

"I was so green," he continued, "nobody could believe it wasn't an act. I mean here was this kid, just out of UCLA, didn't know Ruscha from his own asshole, harbored no ambition for making art or selling it, worked a mundane job without complaint, got along with everyone, and so on. Had I declared an ambition I could have diffused all speculation, but because I didn't, everyone—and I didn't realize this until later, of course, at the time I was clueless—wanted to know what my angle was."

"They had no way of knowing what you were up to."

"Right!" He sat up straight. "And frankly, in the long run, neither did I. Last thing I expected was to end up becoming an art dealer."

"You're an art dealer?"

He looked at me surprised. "Of course."

"I didn't know."

"We've got a gallery here, in Chelsea. Plus London and Berlin. That's why I'm trying to get to Germany. For an opening."

One afternoon a few weeks later, as the gallery echoed with the sound of power drivers and the creaking of drywall screws into the wood of sealed crates, Jeff turned to disappoint yet another walk-in visitor through the gap in the partition adjacent to the desk, and saw, in a blur, Francis walk past. He moved across the floor almost silently, in expensive leather loafers, taking no notice of Jeff. Smaller in stature than Jeff remembered, seemingly made of pure muscle but not bulky in the least, as if he had been cut from a giant cable, he moved with no wincing, no hesitation, no distress. He wore a linen suit, no tie, no glasses. There was no sign at all, to Jeff's eye, that Francis had died and come back to life, had been humbled or transformed by the experience.

Francis ascended the stairs without slowing, calling for Marcus and Andrea before he'd reached the top. Then he was gone. If he'd clocked Jeff at all, it was only to verify that someone was behind the desk.

Jeff's heart was pounding out of his chest. Should he go upstairs and introduce himself? He hadn't yet ventured up there and wasn't sure he would be welcome. Still, he hoped to see more of Francis than this, more than the man making a beeline from the front door to his office. At the very least, he thought he'd get to see the man in action. Actual action, making decisions, employing his famous eye.

That moment came a few days later, while they were installing a solo show of new work by Alex Post, one of the regular artists on FAFA's roster. The gallery was a mess. Crates everywhere, work leaning against the walls, rolls of tape, art movers and installers in white gloves scampering around, tinny music playing from a dilapidated boom box, Marcus and Andrea giving orders and perusing checklists. A number of works had come in later than expected.

Post, an oafish middle-aged man in thick black glasses and coveralls, walked from piece to piece, taking in his work, sometimes asking the opinion of whomever was standing nearby, sometimes staring up at the lights as if they would move for him. He took great care in guiding the installers who were hanging the work, pulling out a tape measure at one point and laying down lines of masking tape. He looked more like a foreman than an artist, and Jeff knew who he was only because he'd seen the postcards announcing the opening. In those, Post was clean-shaven and wearing a collarless silk coat, looking five years younger. Jeff had stared at that postcard during one of his interminable days, wondering what it was that made this man an artist, what drove him to create these monumental abstract works. The glasses and silk jacket made him seem like a sagacious aesthete, someone with access to ancient knowledge and higher realms. The man in front of him wouldn't have looked out of place in the service pit at Jiffy Lube.

Francis appeared at the bottom of the stairs as if he'd floated down them, his leather loafers inaudible under the busy atmosphere of the gallery. Jeff tried to catch his eye, but Francis was already past, heading for Post with arms open. They greeted each other with exaggerated goodwill—hugging and slapping each other on the back. Francis asked if everything was to his liking, and Post said that it was, except the prices. He was concerned that Francis had set the numbers too high. He had heard whispers of a softening in the market, and he didn't want to end up like D.S. over at Gagosian.

The prices were fine, Francis told him. He'd presold a third of the paintings and had buyers lined up for the rest.

"Speaking of which," he said, pointing at the painting visitors would see first when they came around the partition, "we've got to swap this one with one from the other room."

The works were hung in a specific order, Post said.

Francis went into the other room, called for two art movers to bring in the painting he wanted.

The art movers brought out the painting, holding it next to the one already hanging in the prime position.

Both works were large abstract geometrical pieces. Arcs and circles against a neutral background, as if drawn with a giant compass. There was nothing freehand or expressive about the work, the shapes seemingly determined by pure physics, as if describing the outlines of soap bubbles in a matrix.

As far as Jeff was concerned, they were indistinguishable in quality, size, even content. Yet Francis favored one over the other. Here was the eye at work.

Post was shaking his head. The piece couldn't go there. It would be out of order. The show was called *The Rake's Progress*— you couldn't put *Marriage* before *Birth*. It didn't make sense. The more he made his case, the more agitated he became. Francis watched him impassively, then asked if he was finished.

Post cocked his chin at Francis.

"The painting goes here," Francis said. "Or you and it can go to fucking Gagosian. Not that he'd have you."

Post stepped closer. He was at least six inches taller than Francis and probably fifty pounds heavier. Francis didn't budge. Jeff was impressed with this show of strength and with Francis's commitment to his eye, an eye that could discern what was special in that painting. Predisposed to root for Francis, Jeff wanted to tell Alex Post to give up the fight and have faith in his dealer.

Andrea stepped in to make peace. "One could argue that *Marriage* is the perfect opener in terms of its being the apotheosis—"

Post put up his hand. He didn't want to be convinced. He would never be convinced. He would simply give in, because that was what one had to do, he said, when dealing with Francis *Arse*-nault, emphasizing the *Arse* in the name. He spewed a series of expletives at no one in particular and declared that he wouldn't be returning for the gallery opening, so everyone else would have to drink the shit wine without him. He walked out.

Francis watched it all with perfect calm. When Post was gone, he clapped his hands together and told everyone to get back to work. *Marriage* went up on the wall, Francis returned to his office. The eye had won.

Jeff emerged from behind the desk to have a look at the painting himself. He stood before it, trying to figure out what Francis saw in it versus the painting that had hung there, but he couldn't see anything particularly remarkable about it. He dipped into the back gallery to look at *Birth*, which was now hanging where *Marriage* had been. It seemed as good a painting as *Marriage*, in its palette and arrangement of formal elements and general appearance. Jeff wasn't a fan of either of these paintings, but still he felt he should have been able to determine what made *Marriage* exceptional.

Was this what it meant to have the eye? To be able to discern a distinction in quality so subtle as to be invisible to the man on the street? Or was there a secret code, a hidden message visible only to the cognoscenti—a concept Jeff would have understood had he actually majored in art history? It irked him to think that art—he *did* believe in art—could turn into just another thing to make people feel stupid. Because when he admitted it to himself, that was what the painting did, it made him feel that he was missing something. The fact that others saw it, or claimed to, to the degree that one painting was drastically better or more deserving of exposure than another, only underlined for him the cryptic nature of the world into which he'd ventured.

23

A few days later, Jeff noticed Marcus leaving the gallery with a racquet under his arm. He asked Marcus if he was heading out to play tennis. Marcus grinned, and Jeff knew immediately he'd gotten it wrong.

"Squash," Marcus said.

Jeff had heard of squash but had never met anyone who actually played it.

"It's like racquetball, right?"

Marcus was still grinning. "Racquetball is to squash as checkers is to chess. Comprende?"

"Where do you play?"

"Sports Club LA. Francis has a membership."

"You play with Francis?"

"Getting back into it. He broke a few ribs playing a while back. That was why— Nah, that was before your time."

"Against you?"

Marcus shook his head. "I'd never hear the end of it. It was some guy from the club."

Squash. No talk of swimming, or drowning, or CPR, or that brick wall we're all hurtling toward turning out, this time, to have been made of paper. Why had Francis lied? Was he embarrassed? Worried a near drowning would reveal weakness?

"Opening is next week," Marcus said on his way out the door. "You might want to go shopping. Don't skimp on the shoes."

Jeff spent two weeks' pay on an all-black ensemble from Banana Republic and a pair of slip-on loafers from Florsheim.

24

The night of the event, Jeff was put in charge of the music—a CD mix of Charlie Parker tunes, volume low enough to be almost subliminal, but high enough to stave off total silence.

Post slinked in a half hour before the reception, walking the gallery and nodding with approval at the installation, with the exception of *Marriage*, which he pointedly refused to look at. He complained to Francis about the prices again, to which Francis replied that they'd double in the next five years, and this constituted their kiss and make up, after which the artist prevailed on the bartender to open a bottle of pinot grigio.

The imperious and implacable Francis, the one who had dominated Alex Post, was gone. This opening-night Francis emanated an aura of generosity. His smiles were genial and wide, and his wineglass was always full—he sipped only if someone toasted. He made up for his small stature by always standing under one of the large hanging lights, which were organized in a sort of grid, attached to cables from the ceiling. He didn't stay in one place, but when he moved, he invariably ended up directly below one of the lights, a tungsten glow illuminating his hair. Andrea and Marcus moved purposefully through the crowd, bringing people to Francis and ordering the assistants around, but Francis himself seemed to exist above it all, unflappable and serene.

Jeff noticed, once the reception was in full swing, that the crowd's din, the talking and coughing and laughing, oscillated, growing louder as people tried to talk over one another, and then, according to some principle he couldn't understand, descended in volume, only to go through the cycle again. That nadir in volume was when the music could be heard, for a moment, before conversation covered it again.

There wasn't much looking at the art. The guests were there
to be seen . . . by the other guests, Jeff supposed. He didn't recognize anyone. But he noticed that some, the more powerful ones,
presumably, were always approached by others, whereas another
group did most of the approaching, in a regular pattern. A third
group—the hoi polloi, as much as they could be called that in this
context—limited their interactions to the people they'd arrived
with. They were also the only ones looking at the art. Who were
they? Would-be artists, assistants, appraisers, print dealers, cubicle
jockeys from the auction houses . . .

Jeff walked the galleries, making sure he was always looking
as though he was on his way somewhere, taking in whatever conversations he could, and keeping an eye on Francis, the central
cog in this complex and glittering machine. It was seductive, the
machine. Enchanting. He couldn't help but be swayed and impressed.

As a hedge against intimidation, he reminded himself that
if he hadn't saved Francis's life, none of this would have been
happening.

Andrea shuttled an older Middle Eastern man toward *Marriage*, and Marcus simultaneously alerted Francis. The whole
night, this was the only time Jeff had noticed Francis moving for
someone else. They greeted each other with handshakes and
smiles, more formal than usual for Francis. The man seemed
pleased by the painting, and he and Francis stood shoulder to
shoulder in front of it discussing its merits, presumably, though
Jeff wasn't within earshot.

Marcus caught him gawking. "He's an Al-Thani," he said, as if
that should mean anything to Jeff. "Relative of the Qatari emir."

Jeff felt he was witnessing a moment of some import.

"Francis is showing him the best painting," Jeff said, under
his breath.

"The best?"

"He moved it there, to the prime spot," Jeff said.

Marcus looked at him like he'd just stepped off a tractor.

"Mr. Al-Thani already owns the painting," he said. "Purchased it sight unseen last week. A wedding gift for his future daughter-in-law."

Of course. *Marriage.*

25

"How did that affect your opinion of Francis?" I asked.

Jeff smiled. "I was disillusioned. It didn't obviate the eye, but it did piss me off, how he railroaded the artist in favor of a collector. I didn't yet know what I know today."

"Meaning?"

"The art is only the glue. It's not always just glue, obviously. Sometimes it's capital-*A* art. But for the most part, the work, from the perspective of the art world, exists to provide an occasion for buying and selling, for socializing, for crowing, for telegraphing taste, for cleaning up dirty money."

"I'm sure the artists don't see it that way," I said.

"Some do, some don't."

I raised my eyebrows.

"Every once in a while artists try to come up with work that can't be bought or sold. But the market always finds a way."

His eyes grew distant. He asked me if I wanted another non-alcoholic beer. I offered to get drinks this time, since I needed to hit the restroom anyway.

"Vodka soda, please," he said.

I made my way through the lounge's maze of tables and small rooms until I found, tucked away, the restrooms. They were utterly unlike the ones downstairs: marble everywhere, orchids on the counters, disposable hand towels, and an overriding sense of space and serenity. No line, no crowd, no suitcases crammed into stalls populated by groaning defecators. The doors here went from floor to ceiling. It wasn't as fancy as a luxury hotel, but it was—as the bathrooms in the rest of the airport were not—humane. I urinated in peace, absorbing the meditative music coming from speakers in the ceiling.

I didn't know what to make of Jeff's story so far. I was still di-
gesting the fact that he'd become an art dealer. Was that what lay
behind his years-long reticence? Or was there more? As his story
proceeded, I felt an increasing indefinable discomfort, perhaps
stemming from the knowledge that I was the first auditor, the
accidental confessor who by my mere appearance had spurred
on this excavation of his past. Was it excavation, though, Jeff getting everything off his chest? Or was he painting for me a kind
of self-portrait? And what is a self-portrait if not self-serving? The
tale of the young, ingenuous Jeff stumbling his way into FAFA
could have, in another telling, come off as sinister. Based on what
I'd heard thus far, I could have easily and justifiably accused Jeff
of stalking Francis Arsenault.

I washed my hands and headed to the bar. The morose bartender, with feathered blond hair and an almost-handlebar
mustache, looked like he'd stepped out of the late 1970s.
When I ordered Jeff's vodka soda and my nonalcoholic beer,
he perked up.

"You're the one drinking the near beers," he said.

I nodded.

"Your friend there is quite the talker."

"That he is."

"I had an ex like that. Wasn't happy unless my head was full
of her words."

I put a couple of dollars into the tip jar and made my way back
toward our table.

Jeff sat leaning forward, his elbows on the armrests of his
chair, his mouth resting on his interlaced hands, as though he
was praying, or deep in thought.

The moment he saw me in his peripheral vision, he popped
upright, animated and reaching for his drink.

After I sat down, he held up his glass.

"A toast," he said, "to serendipity."

"You mean that we bumped into each other?" I asked.

"Sure," he said.

"Or are you talking about the past?"

He shrugged. "Why not both?"

We sipped our drinks, and Jeff resumed his story.

26

Marcus buzzed Jeff's extension.

"I need you to help Fiona with a project," he said.

Jeff had no idea who Fiona was. He ascended the private stairs with a tightness in his throat. He would soon be, he thought, in close proximity to Francis, maybe afforded the opportunity to finally have a conversation with him. He imagined himself coming out with it, telling Francis he had saved his life. What would the fallout be? Lose the job, get a reward? At the top of the stairs was a small waiting room, with a white sofa and a coffee table covered with catalogues from old shows. A hallway led to offices, and he realized that this space existed above the shipping room and the small back gallery room, which had a lower ceiling than the rest of the gallery.

At the end of the hall, Francis's door was open. Andrea stood in the doorway, asking his opinion of the depth of the pockets of a certain collector. Jeff could just barely see Francis sitting at his desk.

Marcus poked his head out of the closest door and invited Jeff inside. Marcus sat across from a middle-aged woman, red hair with bangs, deep-set eyes. In profile, she looked mannish. There was nothing "art world" about her. The way she dressed, she could have been the college counselor at a large public high school.

"This is Fiona," said Marcus. "Our registrar. She knows more than anyone about what goes on here. Where the works come from, where they go, for how much. She knows where the bodies are buried, and how deep."

Jeff smiled and shook her hand.

"Are you back from a break?" he asked.

She looked at him, puzzled. "No, I've been here," she said.

He couldn't help but marvel at the fact that despite having

worked at the gallery for over a month he'd never seen her before. Had she walked past him without his noticing? Or come in earlier and left later? And why had he never heard her name in the regular gossip about the gallery's employees and artists? Her invisibility unsettled Jeff, as if by not participating in the hierarchical skirmishes of the gallery, she was declaring supreme power.

She explained that she was in the process of digitizing the gallery's records, and that Marcus had suggested they also digitize the Rolodex. She asked Jeff if he knew how to use Microsoft Excel. He said he did, though he'd never used it. He was confident he could figure it out.

He was handed a laptop and the Rolodex.

"You can work at your desk," Marcus said.

Jeff left Marcus's office, casting a glance down the hall toward Francis's. The door was closed.

He spent much of the day going through the Rolodex, entering names, phone numbers, and addresses. Some had businesses attached to them—other galleries, art consultants, auction houses—but many were just a name and a phone number. Jeff knew none of them, other than an actor here and there. Steve Martin, for instance. Looking back, it was hard to imagine that he could have read those names, *typed* them out letter by letter, and have had no associations go off in his mind, no clue about their profile, their wealth, their tastes, their eccentricities, their desires, their insecurities, their weaknesses . . .

Shortly after lunch he was typing an entry when he heard shouting upstairs. Francis.

"Why the fuck didn't you take care of it when I was traveling?" was all Jeff heard clearly.

Then Marcus apologizing, offering to do something, Jeff couldn't make out what.

"I'll take care of it myself, thank you," Francis said.

He came padding down the stairs in his leather loafers. Jeff cast a smile in his general direction, looking for acknowledgment.

Only when Francis was more or less on top of him did he realize that he was coming to his desk.

"Can I help?" Jeff asked.

Francis reached across Jeff, putting his body between him and the desk, directly blocking his line of sight, no apology, no "Excuse me," and grabbed the Rolodex, as if Jeff had been just another piece of furniture. Then he pitter-pattered back up the stairs.

27

"I could smell him. His coffee breath. The soap he used, the sweat, the fabric of his jacket. He was right *there*." Jeff put his hand in front of his face. "I could have taken a bite. He was in my space. You know, you're a writer, that space between your eyes and the screen, just above your half-outstretched forearms, that's *your* space. It's your biome, or whatever they're calling it. It is self, not other. And there he was, in it, crossing it, violating it, *without a word*. As if he was entitled to it. Or, more than that, as if it didn't exist. As if I were the chair. An object. And the problem, the old problem, presented itself to me anew. The surface! I was literally as close as I could have been to Francis, but what had it gotten me? Nothing. Who the fuck was Francis? How would I know? Was he heroic? Troubling? No man is a saint, right? I didn't think I'd saved a saint, I hadn't expected to, everyone has their flaws. I wanted him to be good, though, I wanted to feel that I had done a good thing not only for him but for all the people he came in contact with."

Jeff sat on the edge of his chair, spoke with agitation, as if plunged back into the scenes he was recounting. I envied his faith in language, in memory. For him there seemed to be no distance between what he was recounting and what had happened. He was as engaged in it as an actor on a stage, completely tuned into the vivid illusion he was creating for his audience.

"The problem with working at FAFA was that I was so low on the totem pole, I might as well have been invisible. I had been provided with physical proximity, but it wasn't enough to over-come the institutional distance.

"I needed to get the old man's attention. Bring in a collector, set up a deal. All schemes going round in my naive little head, but where to start? I had no idea. Less than no idea. All I could do was look and listen and make myself indispensable to FAFA and, therefore, to Francis."

"There were many things you could have done."

"Time was cheap then. I had nothing but time. And if I discovered that understanding Francis Arsenault inside and out was impossible, well, then, I would cross that bridge . . . But we never really know anyone, do we?"

He stirred the last of his drink, mostly ice, with his finger.

"I mean you could have let it go."

He shook his head. "You have to understand, it was all I had."

"Did you get the Rolodex back?" I asked.

He nodded. "Fiona brought it down a half hour later. 'Don't mind Francis,' she said, as if she were talking about the bad behavior of a seven-year-old.

"I made my way through the names, addresses, numbers, doing my best to be accurate, distracting myself from the drudgery of data entry by speculating about whose names I was looking at. Some were stickier than others. With those I felt like I could evoke the person from the name. They summoned for me visions of wealth and excess, institutional power, toadyism, or even carnality, as if a name itself could denote fuckability.

"I don't remember them all now, of course, but over the years I had the chance to meet quite a few of them, those names for whom I had created ages, looks, lives . . . And do you know what the correlation turned out to be, between who these people were and who I imagined them to be, based on their names?"

I shrugged.

He made a zero with his fingers and thumb.

"I'm telling you. I didn't know a damn thing about anything."

"So you've said."

28

Sometime later Jeff went to an opening at PaceWildenstein, on the other side of Beverly Hills. He had trouble figuring out where it was, since he'd walked over and was on the Wilshire side of the building, where the facade was dominated by a Niketown. He entered the Niketown and asked the guy behind the register if he knew where he could find the PaceWildenstein gallery, and the guy shrugged. Someone overheard, though, a customer, and she told him to go around back. He did so, and found a brick driveway active with valet parkers and various art people making their way inside. It seemed odd to him, the building being divided into a Niketown and an art gallery, both spaces cavernous enough to comprise the whole mass of the building, as if Niketown and PaceWildenstein occupied the same space, but only one or the other could be experienced depending on the observer's position.

The opening was like the one at FAFA, but larger and with better wine. The artist was Agnes Martin. She stood in the middle of the room, wearing a muumuu of natural fibers, her short gray hair looking like she'd cut it herself. People approached her with reverence, because of her age, Jeff thought. He didn't think much of the work, square paintings with baby blue and pink horizontal lines on them. He wondered if she'd run out of time before the show.

He recognized some faces in the crowd, people who had come to the FAFA opening, no doubt a number of them appearing in Francis's Rolodex, but he didn't know any of them, so he tried to find a way to occupy himself until Marcus or Andrea arrived. He got himself a cup of wine and, for lack of anything else to do, made his way around the room looking at the paintings. Up close, the attention to detail was more apparent, but he couldn't fathom why they had been made, and why people would be interested in them. Even more than what was hanging at FAFA, these works puzzled and irritated him.

He was into his second cup of wine when he became aware of a young woman standing next to him, looking at the same painting. In his peripheral vision, he noticed her stealing a glance at him. He cleared his throat and asked her what she thought. She asked him what he thought. He said he asked her first. She said that her name was Chloe. He introduced himself. She asked if he'd been at the FAFA opening. He said yes. She said she thought she'd seen him before.

She was a senior at USC, majoring in fine art and art history. She'd come to the show because she was "interested," she said. While they talked he tried to size her up. She wasn't dressed like a college student, or at least any that he'd known at UCLA. She wore a designer dress, simple, black, and long, with spaghetti straps. She wasn't wearing an excessive amount of makeup, but she'd spent time in front of the mirror. Her hair was dishwater blond, cut in a style popular from television at the time.

She seemed both interested in him and distracted by whatever was going on behind him, like she was trying to do two things at once. He hated when people looked around the room while they talked with you, looking for someone better or more important. He turned and looked over his shoulder, trying to see what she was so interested in, but he couldn't figure out what it was. Perhaps she was avoiding someone, he thought, using him as a shield.

Then she took his hand and asked him to come with her. Next thing he knew, they were standing in front of Agnes Martin, flanked on either side by gallery people. Chloe stepped forward, shook Agnes's hand, congratulated her on the show. Her confidence was strange. Jeff couldn't put his finger on it, she didn't seem to know Agnes Martin, and Agnes Martin made no sign that she knew Chloe. And yet Chloe felt utterly entitled to step into the center of everything to pay her respects to the artist.

Chloe stepped to the side and gestured at Jeff.

"And this is Jeff," she said, "Cook. Jeff Cook," as if introducing a person of import.

Agnes Martin turned her eyes to Jeff. She had a wrinkled face and pursed mouth, eyebrows slightly raised. Her look, to Jeff, was one of doubt or worry, as if it pained her to meet him. He put out his hand, said it was nice to meet her. She shook his hand but instead of letting go, she brought up her other hand and held his hand between hers. She stared into his eyes as if she were trying to read his mind. He was totally unprepared for her intensity and smiled involuntarily. She blinked a few times and said something like "My pleasure," or "Yes," or "Nice to meet you as well," and let go of his hand and broke the gaze.

"I had no clue who she was," Jeff said. "Knew nothing about her artistic credo, her hermit-like life, her status in the art world. I knew only what I saw in front of me, which was an elderly woman painting in blues and pinks. I figured she'd had a tiny stroke while shaking my hand.

"Only later, once I learned a thing or two, once my appreciation for her work grew to match—and even surpass—her reputation, once I'd spent time with her writings, did I look back at that meeting and feel what I feel today."

"Which is what?"

He leaned forward, lowered his voice.

"She knew."

"What did she know?"

"Things I couldn't have foreseen. She touched me and stared into my eyes as if she were meeting the Dalai Lama. She saw something in me. I was a fellow traveler, marked for an uncommon life."

"You really believe that?" I asked.

He shrugged. "Sometimes I do."

He and Chloe went out after the opening, to Kate Mantilini. They sat in a booth with a window looking onto Wilshire Boulevard. They ate and drank and talked, pausing only when a fire truck or ambulance passed outside. Chloe crossed herself every time but made a point of saying she wasn't religious—it was a habit leftover from her Catholic school days.

They went back to his house, the actor's house. She complimented him on it immediately, throwing a jacket over a chair as if she lived there, and he told her he was house-sitting. Her eyes scanned the room, taking in the various antiques and artifacts of the actor's travels around the world. For a friend in Vancouver, Jeff continued, who's the regular house sitter. He explained that the house belonged to an actor who had multiple homes and was currently off shooting somewhere, New Orleans or London or someplace. She wandered over to a series of pictures hanging in the hallway.

"Don't tell me this is *his* house," she said, saying the actor's name.

"You've got to tell me the actor's name," I said.

"I promised Dylan I wouldn't tell anyone."

"That was years ago."

"Fair enough. It was Brad Pitt."

"Holy shit," I said. "That's huge."

"That's exactly what she said."

"Holy shit," Chloe said. "That's huge."

"I guess," Jeff said.

"At least let me look around. I mean, this kilim is astonishing. And where do you get a lamp like this?"

Chloe didn't know, she couldn't have known, that she was running roughshod over the stories he and G had created around these objects, the imaginary world they'd drummed up, just the two of them, for their own benefit, a world in which the house was theirs, the memories had all been laid down, the roots had grown into the soil, and they were adults, real adults, bandying around names for future offspring. She was, by her mere presence, but also with her eye, cutting it to ribbons.

He welcomed it.

Jeff gave her a tour of the house, every room, and she couldn't disguise her excitement at this being Brad Pitt's house, at these being his things, and while she walked from room to room she no doubt imagined him inhabiting the house, walking from room to room himself, running lines or snorting lines or whatever it was that actors did with their days and nights. As she and Jeff walked through, looking at the same objects and spaces, each of them saw something completely different in this house that was not theirs, each of them walked not only through the physical edifice with its physical decor but also through a second house in the mind, an image of a house, the image that makes a house into a home, and in fact it was impossible to see the house accurately, it was impossible for both of them to see the same house, a condition that was only exacerbated by the emotionally charged overlays, hers excitement at finding herself in Brad Pitt's home, his a negative form of nostalgia, a painful recollection of another time, which in and of itself consisted of he and G creating, cocreating, consciously and fictionally, what the house would mean to them, as if by agreement, so that they might, when occupying it, see the same thing for once, or as close as was possible for two separate individual consciousnesses to share the vision of a place.

Upstairs, in the master bedroom, Chloe oohed and aahed over the Jacuzzi tub and steam shower. She moved from one detail to another rapidly, with an energy he hadn't seen at the gallery or restaurant. In his gut he felt G trying to assert herself over the territory, or his memory of G, as he untangled the synapses no longer corresponding to the real-world situation. He followed Chloe into the walk-in closet, prepared to hear more oohs and aahs—it was a massive closet, with an island in the middle, glass top, drawer for ties and jewelry—but she was silent. She hesitated for a moment just inside the closet. Jeff assumed it had stunned her into silence. He was right behind her. She turned around as if she'd decided she'd had enough, or for some reason couldn't take anymore, as if the closet had exhausted or overwhelmed her. That was his immediate impression at her stopping short and turning quickly, before he'd had a chance to get out of the way, so that they were face-to-face, or almost face-to-face—he was slightly taller than she was. Before he could turn or step aside to let her pass, she took his wrist in her hand, tilted her chin up, and kissed him on the lips, not a peck, lingering there, parting his lips with hers, until the kiss transformed into a full-on passionate kiss, one hand still on his wrist, her other hand on the back of his neck, to ensure, it seemed, that he wouldn't stop kissing her until she was done kissing him. Eventually she put both hands on the sides of his head and pulled away, locking her eyes on his.

"I got tired of waiting," she said.

Her energy had changed again. She had kissed him, and he had kissed back. She seemed to have shed the excited, nervous energy she'd arrived with, the bouncing from one of Brad Pitt's things to another, the mania with which she had seemed to be devouring the house with her eyes. Now they were on the same wavelength. When they kissed again, all the cognitive dissonance and G thoughts faded, and he simply wanted more Chloe.

33

"In the morning, I drove her to her car, which was still parked in the PaceWildenstein/Niketown lot. The overnight fee was staggering, I asked her if I could cover half, but she didn't care. She had a cute little BMW, late model. I remember thinking USC, BMW, what am I getting myself into here? She didn't seem to mind my old Volvo, though, which I took as a good sign that she was okay slumming it with me. It was only as we were saying goodbye that we realized we didn't have a way to get in touch, so we swapped phone numbers."

"As one does," I said.

"So I'm writing down her number, and I ask her for her last name, and she asks me if I know a lot of Chloes. I say that she's the only one. She says that, in that case, I don't need her last name. She was very smiley, you know, flirtatious as she said this, and I could tell it was to cover up a degree of reluctance on her part. I start in with 'What is it, Chloe Mussolini? Chloe Manson?' Goofing off, making a bit of fun of her for holding back her last name but also burning with curiosity, especially because she's not playing along. She looks genuinely worried at this point, no sign of the flirtatious Chloe. Honestly, I couldn't figure out why. 'How bad can it be?' I said, and she said, 'Don't hate me.'"

"Hate her?"

"That's what she said."

"Why would you hate her?"

"Well, turns out her last name is . . . Arsenault."

"No."

Jeff nodded. "She knew I worked for her father. She first saw me at the FAFA opening. She thought I was attractive, but she wasn't going to approach me while I was working. She sort of just noted my presence. Then, when she saw me at PaceWildenstein, she felt like she'd been given a second chance, and she wasn't about to pass it up. That was when she appeared next to me, looking at the Agnes Martin painting. She said she had to make sure, one, that I wasn't gay, and two, that I could hold an actual conversation, and then, she thought, she would let me know, full disclosure, who she was. But she couldn't seem to find the right time. She was worried it would make things weird, and she was having fun. Then, she went to my place, and we hooked up, and she knew she'd blown it by not telling me earlier, in fact she was on the verge of waking me up to tell me, but decided against it.

"So she had been keeping a secret from me from the start. But as soon as she divulged her secret, I was burdened with a secret of my own. It was as if she'd handed it off to me. I could see the burden lifted from her conscience. She'd kept her secret for one night. I'd keep mine, what? Forever?

"Reading my face she knew I'd been thrown off-balance. She had no idea how much. I kept having to remind myself that from her perspective it was only an awkward situation, an instance in which my job might be threatened. She sensed my reaction, my strong reaction, she had a good intuitive sense, and she worried that she'd blown it. She knew right away, she told me, how important the job was for me. And how much I feared her father—everyone did. I wasn't alone in that. She assured me that we could keep 'us' secret, that she wouldn't out me, that dating me had nothing to do with the fact that I worked at FAFA. That even if we split up, she wouldn't narc on me."

"Feared her father?" I asked.

"We'll get to that. I listened to her reassurances and watched her face. I had thought that this thing with Chloe could be a new chapter for me, you know, whisk me away from the bundle of everything else, the loss of G, what happened at the beach, the whole Francis thing. I had fantasized that I might find my way out by filling my head and heart with something else. Was that a thought I'd had in the middle of the night, with Chloe at my side?

That's how I remember it. But then, to discover that what I had seen as my potential escape hatch had, through no planning or forethought on my part, led me right back to Francis?"

There it was again, no planning or forethought.

"I didn't turn away. I could have easily and justifiably done it, given her some excuse, told her that I couldn't risk my job by dating her, but the thing was, I liked her. I really did. This would not be a one-night-stand situation. That wasn't my style."

He shook his head, as if marveling at the vicissitudes of his own story.

"You kept seeing her?"

He nodded slowly.

"Our relationship developed under a cloud of paranoia. We ordered in rather than going out. When we did meet out in the world, we avoided anywhere that we might bump into anyone we knew. This might have seemed like overkill, but it was also fun, one of the games we played. A relationship needs its games—if there's no sense of play, there's only desperation, fear of being alone. I loved that we had a game, known only to us. Sometimes we rented movies, but more often, we talked. Since I was working full-time and she was on a student's schedule, we usually ended up at my place, Brad Pitt's house. Plus, at her place there was a roommate, a young woman I hardly ever saw, very studious, always cooped up in her room. One night while we were watching a movie in her living room, Chloe insisted that we have sex on the sofa. I went along with it, but I couldn't help but think of her roommate, trapped in her room. I asked her whether the roommate was home, and she said that if she was, she wasn't coming out now. This shocked me, you know, it seemed very inconsiderate. But I suppose she was a chip off the old block in some ways. After that night I avoided going to her place.

"Chloe was one of those people who go after everything they want, without hesitation and without calculating the potential challenges. Because that wasn't something I did readily, I saw it as a sign of maturity rather than what it was, which was the result of a lifetime of entitlement."

"She was spoiled."

He laughed. "She wasn't used to hearing the word *no*, I'll put it that way. She moved through the world as if she would never have to."

"She hadn't suffered any massive blows."

"She had been protected from those."

"By her parents?"

"By Francis, more than by her mother. She loved her father, she assured me, but there was great ambivalence there. She recognized him as a vanguard in his field, as the provider, as the daddy who had given her everything she'd ever wanted, who'd taken her on trips with him, and so on. But since she'd left the house, she'd begun to see things that hadn't been obvious to her when she was younger and living with them. And his behavior toward her had changed. He insisted on her coming home for dinner every Sunday night, even if he was out of town. He was constantly adjusting her spending money up and down. He threatened, at one point, to stop paying her tuition, over a minor disagreement. He loved her, she knew he did, but her leaving home had made him more controlling.

"When he couldn't take it out on her, he took it out on her mother, an extremely talented artist whose career had been scuttled, in Chloe's estimation, by both the demands of motherhood and domination by Francis, who, while touting his support for her art, was always in some way undercutting it.

"That had all started when they first got together—Francis had been a fan of Alison's work and went for a studio visit. He fell for her immediately, and she was drawn to his energy, what she perceived as a sense of fun and I would argue was a deep-seated need for constant stimulation. Her discovery that he wanted both to date her and show her work felt like a double bounty. She couldn't have known, in those days, that one could cancel out the other, that she could be accused of sleeping her way to the top (before she had gotten anywhere near the top), that her beauty would be a handicap, that people would never see her work and not think of her as *the girlfriend of,* then *the wife of.* She had minor success, a few sales to real collectors, but she soon realized that it was contingent on her being with Francis. People couldn't see her work, even when it was right in front of them. What they saw was potential to curry favor with the dealer.

"At one point, this was after Chloe was in school full-time, Alison showed a body of work at a different gallery, under a pseudonym. Of course, the gallerist knew who she was and was doing her a favor, and Francis was in on it, but otherwise nobody knew. The show didn't sell well. There was no track record, no persona to attach the work to. It was good stuff, but *on its own merits* it didn't rise above the glut of other work out there."

"The market isn't the only indicator of artistic quality."

"It wasn't only that the show didn't sell. It wasn't reviewed. It had zero impact. The idea she'd had, that the work could go out into the world purified of everything attached to her other work, was naive, and she should have realized it, but she took the failure of this venture as a sign that everyone had been right, that she had not been a distinguished artist but an average one, one who happened to have a pretty face and a powerful husband."

"But in reality, how much work would stand up to that test?" I asked. "I mean work by highly successful contemporary artists."

"Almost none. Alison refused to see it, at least with relation to her own work, but Chloe understood it. She had an innate understanding of her father's world. She tried to convince her mother that the test had been impossible, that her work was wonderful, that she had to ignore the downside of her association with Francis and enjoy the upside. But her mother wouldn't budge. The failure of the pseudonymous show was to her an incontestable verdict. Which, ironically, you could take as an indicator that she was a real artist. Artists, good ones, real ones, always take criticism seriously, even personally, and reject praise. If the work sucks, it's their fault. If it's brilliant, credit goes to the gods.

"She went into design. Founded a successful interior design business. A field in which her association with Francis was unquestionably useful. She claimed to be happy, but Chloe thought otherwise. One doesn't stop being an artist. She had given up on her dreams. This was something Chloe had promised herself she would never do. I believed her, you know, she was very convincing. I didn't have many dreams of my own, other than an abstract idea of not wanting to go backward, you know, not wanting to live in a shack in Santa Cruz with my mother. I didn't have any big dreams to give up on. I've always been more of a regular guy. I guess what I did have, what I prided myself on, was my integrity."

"The guy who returns the blanket."

"Sure, also the guy who thinks there's more to life than money."

"That was all of us in those days."

34

Jeff was working at the gallery one morning, sitting at the desk, putting address labels on postcards, when Marcus appeared next to him, a serious look on his face.

"He wants to see you."

Marcus looked up and nodded his chin as if referring to God.

"I'll watch the desk," he said. And then, with what sounded like kindness, he wished Jeff good luck.

Jeff had been keeping his eyes and ears open, vis-à-vis Francis. This consisted mainly of watching him arrive and leave, yell at someone upstairs, and, occasionally, walk a collector through the gallery. Nothing had changed, in other words, and he and Francis remained strangers to each other.

His major source for Francis-related information was Chloe. Through her he was getting a clearer picture of the man he'd rescued. Possibly even a clearer picture than Francis had of himself, in some ways.

The problem was that Chloe hardly ever described the same Francis. One day he was a control-obsessed, domineering, personality-quashing monster. Another day, a loving, supportive, providing, beneficent king. Jeff asked leading questions, like "Has he always been like this?" Trying to figure out how the near drowning had affected him. At one point she mentioned a recent crisis, that after he hurt himself playing squash—she had been fed the same story as everyone at the gallery . . . or knew otherwise and wasn't saying—he went out and bought himself a Porsche.

"How obvious is that?" she asked, incredulous. The inimitable Francis Arsenault, doing what every fifty-year-old man of means would do. Like *a regular person.*

Now Jeff had to walk upstairs and face the man himself. He

couldn't imagine why Francis would want to see him. They had not yet had an actual conversation. Jeff took each step slowly and carefully, his hand on the railing to temper the incipient dizziness. This was what he'd signed up for, wasn't it? But now it had been complicated by what was happening with Chloe.

He made his way down the hall to the door at the end. It was open. Francis sat leaning back in his chair, feet up on his desk, phone to his ear. He waved Jeff in and gestured for him to sit. Behind him hung a large painting, a square canvas, dark, with a large bright circle of gold leaf at the center. And, as if a shadow had been cast on it, the outline of a head and neck in black in the circle. As Jeff looked at the painting, he felt that he recognized it, then he remembered. It had been in one of the articles he'd found at UCLA. In black and white he hadn't realized that it was gold. Also, in the portrait, Francis had been sitting up, his head filling the negative space in the gold circle, so that he looked like Jesus from one of those old paintings. In Francis's current position, he left the work unobscured, the void unfilled, so that the shadow denoted an absence.

Francis barked into the phone. "Some people buy with their eyes, and some people buy with their ears. This guy buys with his ears. And he's a dead end, a sinkhole. This thing is going to go into his apartment on the Upper West Side and be seen by nobody but his maid, his dog, and his future ex-wife. If we're lucky. So much shit in storage. You give this guy a good painting, you might as well throw it out the window. No, no, sure, they're all good. But some are less good than others. Sell him one of those. Ears." And with that, he hung up.

He looked at Jeff. There was the drooping eyelid. The gaze. The eye. Jeff felt a chill run up his spine. He didn't dare speak first.

"You're not an idiot," Francis said.

"No, sir," Jeff said.

"I thought you might be," Francis continued, "with that lost-puppy look on your face. One of those pretty boys we put up front to avoid being accused of only putting pretty girls up there."

"No, sir," Jeff repeated, painfully aware that he was currently wearing the lost-puppy look on his face.

"These extra fields," Francis said, turning his laptop around to face Jeff. "You did this?"

Jeff scanned the screen. It was the database he'd created from the Rolodex. While transcribing the information, he'd found a whole bunch of extra marks, scattered scribbles, codes. Marginalia. Not wanting to lose that data in the transition, he created a few extra fields in the database to contain the information: AlphaNum (for the alphanumeric codes); Artists (for those who had artist names scribbled next to them); and Notes (for anything else).

"Yes, sir," Jeff said. "I wanted to make sure everything went into the database."

Francis turned the laptop around again. He pulled a pair of readers off the desk and put them on, settling them on the tip of his nose. He then took a pen from the desk and started chewing on the end.

"Those notes, those codes," he said. "They're more important than the phone numbers and addresses. Anyone can find a fucking phone number. That extra information, that is the most important stuff, the fruit of years of cultivation. And you thought to put it into the database. Very clever. Because that information exists only in one other place." He tapped his temple with the pen. "And there's no transcribing what's in here. That goes where I go."

"And when," Jeff felt compelled to add.

"When what?"

"When you go."

Francis looked at him strangely, as if recognizing him for the first time. Jeff wondered if he was remembering the encounter by the hotel elevators. He couldn't possibly be remembering what happened at the beach, could he?

"Tell me about yourself," Francis said.

Jeff laid out a few biographical details. Santa Cruz, single mom, UCLA, worked for a startup.

"Young and ambitious," Francis said wistfully.

"I wouldn't say—"

"Thing about having a smart kid around," he said, "they're a real asset to the business, until they're not. And when they're not, it's because they're plunging the knife into your back."

"That's not what I'm about, I can assure you," he said.

"Give it time. Meanwhile, keep your eyes and ears open. I might have more work for you. If you can figure out how to wipe that look off your face."

The meeting was over, such as it was. Jeff thanked Francis and headed for the door. Marcus would be getting impatient. He hated manning the front desk.

"One more thing," Francis said.

Jeff turned.

"If you break her heart, I'll destroy you."

"He knew?" I asked. "How did he know?"

"To this day I'm not sure. Someone must have seen us, or heard me talking to her on the phone, or caught sight of one of our emails to each other. And I hadn't yet learned how information moves in a business like that, a business predicated on knowing things others did not. Whoever tipped off Francis was no doubt rewarded."

"But how would Francis know whether the information was good?"

"He checked with Chloe first."

"She didn't give you a heads-up?"

"He told her that if she did, he would fire me immediately. She explained that to me later. He wanted to keep me in the dark."

"That's messed up," I said, "putting her in that situation."

"That was Francis, as I was learning."

"But there was an implied approval too, right? I mean he didn't say, 'Don't date my daughter.' "

"Had nothing to do with me. He knew what kind of person his daughter was. She wouldn't kick anyone to the curb on his orders."

At the front desk, Marcus gave him a long, searching look. He wasn't fired, so he must have been moving up. Jeff gave Marcus a look too. Was he the one who had ratted him out?

From that moment on, their interactions simmered with mutual suspicion. Whatever trust they'd established had been premised on Jeff being a lowly assistant and Marcus the highest power to which he could report.

Word spread quickly. Jeff wasn't quite sure how. Within a few days, everyone in the gallery knew about him and Chloe. Jeff sensed that he'd risen, that he was no longer someone who could be inconsequentially ignored. He sensed, too, that he was perceived as an opportunist and a carpetbagger.

None of this bothered him particularly deeply, this underlying narrative that he was fucking his way to the top, mainly because, unbeknownst to all of them, he wasn't angling for a better position. He was more or less devoid of ambition with relation to the gallery, so if he ended up at the top, in his view, it would be purely by happenstance.

37

The Arsenault house, the one they were living in while the Mandeville house was being built, was situated in the grid streets of Santa Monica, north of Montana, where postwar bungalows sat shoulder to shoulder with weathered Spanish colonials, bloated traditionals, Tuscan fantasias, and the occasional Persian palace. It stood out by being modern, or modernish. A small box atop a larger box, rectangular windows gesturing at an international style, it was all light grays and clean lines. Behind it stood an incongruous garage, Spanish-tile roof, old stucco, betraying the house's heritage as decidedly non-modernist while also presumably sheltering Francis's new Porsche.

Jeff sat in his car across the street, watching Chloe and her mother through the large picture window. Chloe had invited him to Sunday dinner, telling him that her mother was dying to meet him. He was trying to gather the courage to go inside, even as he knew that his joining the Arsenaults was a foregone conclusion.

He saw no sign of Francis but wished he had, to prepare himself. He was about to step into an utterly foreign environment—Francis's environment—and subject himself to his scrutiny. How had a string of actions, guileless and improvised, led him here, into the belly of the beast?

He rang the bell. Chloe opened the door. She kissed him and invited him inside, informing him that her father wasn't home yet. They moved into the kitchen, where Chloe poured him a glass of white wine and introduced him to her mother, first name and last name, Alison Baker. Apparently she'd maintained her professional name since her early art-making days.

While they made small talk, Jeff couldn't help but imagine the young Alison Collins Baker, the artist, the one who thought marrying Francis Arsenault might help her career, or at least wouldn't destroy it. He searched her eyes for a hint of sadness, a sign that the young and ambitious artist was in there, hidden behind a curtain, waiting for her cue. But the impression he got, even with the knowledge of her having given up on her dream, was that the Alison Baker before him was a happy and fulfilled woman.

She walked him around the house, making sure he knew it was a rental, showing him a few of the things she'd done with it, pointing out rugs and chairs and pillows. A mirror or two, a pop of color in several of the rooms. She was very much looking forward to decorating the Mandeville house, and she promised to show him the renderings. Chloe seemed less enthusiastic about this, trying to slow her mother down, embarrassed that she seemed to be trying to impress Jeff.

Only after they'd returned to the kitchen and stood around the island refilling their wineglasses did Jeff realize something odd. There was no art on the walls. He mentioned it, and Alison said that they had been living that way a long time. In the early days, they'd had art all over the place, but Francis kept selling it off the walls. She'd fall in love with a piece one day, and the next day it would be in the hands of a collector. After a while, they decided together to keep the art out of the house. Leave the work at the office, she said. As true in that business as in any other.

Jeff asked about her work.

She said that she'd been doing so well lately that she had a seven-month waiting list.

He clarified that he meant her art.

She gave Chloe a quick look.

"Honestly," she said, "this is my art."

She described several jobs they were finishing up, as well as one she was particularly excited about, for a television producer in the Palisades.

"I can't say who, but you'd know his name," she said.

He didn't know anybody's name.

"Basically gave us free rein," she said. "Out with the old and so on."

He had to wonder whether Chloe's view of her mother as an artiste manqué said more about Chloe than the woman who had raised her.

Francis arrived a half hour late. Preoccupied with putting his bags away, he didn't pay Jeff any notice at first. He apologized for being late but said that he had decided to hit the gym after work. His hair was wet, and when he looked to Jeff, cued by Alison, who reminded him that Jeff was joining them for dinner, he locked his eyes on him, and in the instant before smiling and putting out his hand, wore a look of incomprehension that, coupled with the wet hair, shook Jeff to the core.

Jeff felt like he had to defer to Francis's apology, to accept it politely on behalf of everyone else, even as Alison and Chloe seemed annoyed.

"The gym," Jeff said. "Gotta stay fit." And then, caution to the wind: "You a swimmer?"

Another flash from Francis. A millisecond long. A spike of fear as from a trapped animal.

"Squash," Francis said. "I showered afterward. At the gym."

At the gym, he said. It was unnecessary to utter those three words. Anyone would have assumed that he would have showered at the gym. Jeff wondered whether Francis had not been at the gym at all, but in the hotel, with his mistress.

"Doctor said you shouldn't push it," Chloe said.

Francis looked to Alison, who got the message immediately. This was not something to be discussed outside the family.

"Chloe," Alison said. "Pour your father a glass of wine."

Francis shook Jeff's hand firmly, welcomed him into his humble home, as he called it, and smiled openly. He, too, mentioned that it was a rental. There was no hint of the backhanded compliments or veiled threats he'd thrown Jeff's way at the office. This was a more open Francis, a man who seemed pleased with his daughter's choice of boyfriend. The unspoken rule hewed to what Alison had said about the paintings on the wall: work stayed at work.

When they sat down to eat, a fancy bottle of red wine was opened, to go with the tenderloin Alison had prepared. Francis behaved like a king in his little castle, with Alison and Chloe making sure he had what he needed at any given moment. While the food was being plated, Francis and Jeff had a moment together at the table. Francis asked Jeff to remind him where he worked before he came to FAFA. Jeff mentioned the startup, and Francis shook his head.

"Nothing in the art world?"

"Nada," Jeff said.

Francis looked at him, squinting his eyes slightly.

"Did you go to many openings?" he asked.

Jeff, worried that he was being quizzed on his experience, fibbed a little.

"When I could, yes," he said.

"Ahh," Francis said. "That's it, then."

"What?"

"Your face, it's familiar to me. I noticed it when I called you into my office. It's been bothering me since. I had the feeling that I'd seen you before, but I couldn't quite place you."

"You must see lots of people," Jeff said.

"I never forget a painting," Francis said. "And I never forget a face."

During dinner, Jeff was asked for his opinion a few times, in the vein of parents sniffing out the new boyfriend, but for the most part he observed the conversation going on between the Arsenaults.

The dynamic at the table consisted of Francis making ill-informed comments about various things Chloe was doing, or he thought she was doing, in a manner that seemed controlling and overprotective. Alison then chimed in with the reality of the situation, countering Francis's view while also acknowledging the validity of his underlying concerns. Chloe then complained about not being treated like the adult she was. Jeff could have drawn diagrams of their interactions, connecting channels of power, concern, control, money, freedom, and love. They seemed like, to him, who had never been part of one, a normal family.

Occasionally Francis shot him a look of commiseration, but Jeff also caught Francis looking at him out of the corner of his eye, examining him with what might have been an evaluating gaze. Was he envious of Jeff's youth? Thinking about how his life might have gone differently if he were able to backtrack to a point in his early twenties? Or was he still trying to place his face, chasing down the source of that feeling of familiarity?

For his part, Jeff examined Francis too, and not only to assess who he was but also to look for signs of what Chloe had invoked. *Doctor said you shouldn't push it.* Was he in ill health? Was the doctor warning him that what had happened in the ocean could happen again? He knew he couldn't ask about Francis's health, not after Alison's obvious redirection away from the subject, but he could see no sign that the man was anything but hale and hearty.

Francis ate steak and drank wine with gusto. His cheeks were pink, his posture ramrod straight. Despite a long day and a trip to the gym or an assignation in a hotel, he showed no signs of flagging. He was known for his energy, Jeff had heard around the gallery, and he was almost competitive in the way he refilled their wineglasses, as if he and Jeff were engaged in a drinking contest. It felt strange to see Francis, as he drank more, consider Jeff a competitor in anything at all, especially considering their relative positions at FAFA.

At one point Francis knocked over a nearly empty glass of wine, leaving a red splotch on the tablecloth. Alison sprang into action with salt and a paper towel, dabbing up what she could. Francis cursed under his breath, and she assured him that it would come out, then asked him if he wanted her to refill the glass. She approached the spilled wine with no annoyance, no subservience, no fear, but only a soothing calmness. She kissed him on the forehead and looked at him with years-earned fondness. Jeff couldn't help but imagine that face's obverse, what Alison would have looked like mourning Francis's loss.

After the spill, Alison retreated into herself somewhat. At first Jeff thought she might be thinking along the same lines as he was, that if things had gone another way, there would be no Francis at the head of the table. Jeff tossed a joke in her direction a few times, but though she laughed, it was a polite laugh, not the real thing. She remained subdued. Perhaps she was tired, he thought, or had grown tired in the face of Francis's energy, or perhaps the alcohol had had an enervating effect.

Toward the end of the evening, over dessert, Jeff wondered if the cloud hanging over her had nothing to do with fear of losing Francis but instead with the suspicion—or knowledge—that Francis hadn't come from the gym but from a tryst.

There was no way for him to probe this question straight on, but once he and Chloe were in her bedroom—Alison had insisted he sleep over because everyone had had too much to drink—he asked Chloe whether she'd noticed her mom's mood change over the course of the evening. She said she hadn't. This struck him as disingenuous. At the very least, she was engaging in willful blindness. But we do what we can to protect ourselves from the truth.

They made love that night, or had sex, he always wanted to call it making love, but she was very matter-of-fact about it, referring to sex as sex and talking about making sure both of them got off, et cetera. Her frankness was unlike anyone he'd ever dated, and miles away from the romantic trappings with which G had festooned the act. In her unsentimental approach, Chloe was more like a dude, or so it seemed to him, especially on those nights when she would pass out quickly and sleep soundly after they were done.

That night he was hesitant, didn't expect anything to happen. After all, they were in her parents' home, Francis and Alison only a staircase away. But Chloe was in the mood, said a few words about christening the bed. She was drunk and feeling playful. He followed her lead enthusiastically, despite worrying that her parents might hear them, a possibility she seemed not to consider. Maybe it was the thought of her parents hearing them, of Francis hearing them, coupled with the sight of Francis with wet hair, the flashback it had elicited in him, but he couldn't get the rescue out of his mind. He'd push it away, give himself over to Chloe, but it would claw to the front of his attention again, until it finally occurred to him, a thought that had been brewing in there the whole time, that in this moment, he was finally taking his reward.

He was disgusted by the idea.

No, he reminded himself, meeting Chloe had been pure coincidence, a by-product of an entirely separate quest. He had fallen for her. He loved her. She loved him. It was impossible, he told himself, that this had anything to do with his saving Francis, with extracting compensation for granting the man new life. But was it truly impossible? What if, on some level, he was deluding himself, and another part of him, a more elemental part, a more animal part, was working out its own social calculus, in the same way the hierarchy at the art gallery might mimic the hierarchy of a troop of gorillas?

He was, after all, fucking the man's daughter in his own house. Framed that way, the thought so thoroughly repulsed him that it took him out of the moment entirely, and, for the first time in his life, but not the last, his body betrayed him. He chalked it up to the alcohol and made sure Chloe was satisfied otherwise. She fell asleep immediately after. He lay there staring at the ceiling, one leg hanging off the side of the bed to keep the room from spinning, wishing that he could take this moment, he and Chloe in bed, young, drunk, and in love, and zero out everything that had led to it.

"Have you ever wanted to zero out the past?" Jeff asked.

Outside, the lowering sun came in at an angle to the cloud cover, diminishing its power to illuminate the world, and the pot lights in the ceiling gave Jeff a more tired, occasionally sinister look.

"Sure, but—"

"It's impossible." Jeff raised his glass. "I mean, we can drink, but everything comes back in the morning. We have to live with our choices."

"And looking back?" I asked. "*Were you* taking your reward?"

"It's a complicated question," he said, "made only more complicated by what came later."

"Which is what?"

"Like I said before, stick with me."

"Okay, fine, but you're doing well for yourself, or so it seems to me. You've got a wife and a couple of kids. You're traveling the world, in style, representing artists and selling their work. If you could zero out everything that got you here, to this moment, you really would?"

He nodded.

"Everything you've just told me about?"

"Without a second thought," he said.

"What about the feeling of satisfaction, the knowledge that the things in your life were hard won? That sense of your own agency? You'd lose that."

"Gladly," he said.

Having dined with Francis, Jeff felt strange returning to the job, sitting behind the desk, answering the phones, pinging Marcus's extension, doodling on pads, and sorting the mail. The hierarchy had been affected, but he wasn't sure how or whether this would be acknowledged, especially considering the wall Francis had erected between work life and home life. The morning with Chloe had been less fraught, both of them nursing mild hangovers, and in the light of day he had no trouble convincing himself that he was indeed sincere in his feelings for her, that if he had met her on the street, without her being connected to his life in any way, he would still have chosen to be with her, would still be sneaking out of her parents' house with a mug of coffee and a piece of toast in hand. The specter of the selfish and calculating Jeff had receded into the shadows, for the moment at least, and the sense of his own goodness remained intact.

When Francis arrived, he gave Jeff a nod and a "Morning," which he had never done before. Nobody else was around to notice, but to Jeff this represented a tectonic shift in his position at the gallery. He wasn't wrong. A few hours later, Marcus was dispatched downstairs to fetch Jeff for yet another meeting with Francis. When he told him the boss wanted to see him upstairs, he shook his head in an I-don't-know-what-he-sees-in-you kind of way. Jeff shrugged and offered up his chair behind the front desk.

Upstairs, Andrea and Fiona watched him walk down the hall as if he were headed for the gallows, or so it seemed to him. When he entered Francis's office, Francis asked him to shut the door behind him and gestured at a chair opposite his desk. Jeff sat. Francis looked him over.

"You remind me of me when I was your age," Francis said. "I like you."

"Thank you," Jeff said.

"You're not going to disappoint me, are you?"

Jeff shook his head.

Francis laughed. "It was a rhetorical question. Of course you will. It's the way of the world. But in the meantime, let's make something happen. I've got a dinner coming up on Thursday, and I'd like you to join. A few of our artists and collectors. Think you can keep your mouth from hanging open the whole night?"

Jeff had never known his own mouth to hang open.

"The way I see it," Francis continued, "either you've got it or you don't. True for artists, collectors, dealers, everyone. I think you might have it, maybe you don't. Better to find out now than later, and only one way to find out. Sink or swim." If the metaphor rang any bells, his face didn't betray it. "These schmucks out there"—he pointed toward the hallway—"do not have it. Aren't about to get it, either. Don't get me wrong, I love 'em, I mean, they keep the lights on around here, but they are the products of a very specific genus of bureaucracy. They've gotten where they are by applying themselves patiently to a system, they've made their way up the ladder by being careful, being diligent, working hard. It's fine for them, but it's also sad. Because they think it will eventually lead them to the top. Have you ever seen that piece by Abdulrahman Miller? The one with the ladder?"

Jeff shook his head.

"It's a standard-issue ladder, like a wooden thing you'd lean up against a house, and it stands in the center of the room, but it's not leaning on anything. It just goes up and into the ceiling. He secures it to the beams above, then plasters over everything, so it looks like the ladder disappears into the smooth whiteness. In performance, he climbs up, rung by rung, and bumps his head on the ceiling. Then he comes down and does it all over again. And when the performance is over, the ladder stays up in the gallery, and you can see on the ceiling where he was bumping his head, an oily spot on the otherwise white surface. The piece conjures up the glass ceiling, of course, and the limited opportunities for black men in America—he's black—but in my view it also represents the American tendency—the human tendency—to turn everything into fucking ladders, to take the wild, untethered world, always a blink away from chaos, with death staring us down, and instead focus on and put faith in a so-called career path, you know, résumé building, that garbage. I don't mean to diminish the power of experience, experience is essential, but how are you getting it? That's the problem with people who have worked in too many galleries, climbed their way up, not by any brilliance, but by not getting fired, or by making a move—they're all the same person. They think the ladder keeps going, all the way to the top, but it doesn't. Of course, some types are satisfied to do their little part, stop and perch on a rung for the rest of their lives, and they're valuable as hell, bread and butter. But the ambitious ones, they're pathetic, the ladder doesn't go there. It goes into the fucking ceiling. It's no way to live, Jeff. Frankly, I don't understand it."

Francis took a few breaths, aware that he'd gone off on a rant. He didn't apologize. Instead, he trained his eyes on Jeff.

"We get one life. One. And then that's it. There's nothing after. Who wants to spend it on a ladder?"

He waited for a response.

"Not me," Jeff said.

"Right. Not you. I didn't think so. Me either, obviously. But those people out there"—he pointed at the door again, and Jeff wondered whether he meant Marcus and Andrea or the rest of the art world or the world in general—"do it. Every day. They tell each other to keep the faith. What faith? We do what we want, Jeff, or we're nothing."

Jeff didn't think he agreed, but he didn't say anything.

"You're lucky," Francis said. "You've got me to show you the way. I wish I'd had me when I was your age."

"I'm very grateful," Jeff said.

Francis shooed him with his hand. "Oh shut up. Dinner Thursday. Mr. Chow. Eight p.m."

It took Jeff a moment to parse the words, which had sounded to him like a kind of code.

"Dinner," Jeff said.

"For Sasha." Francis's eyes were on his desk. "Shut the door behind you."

Downstairs, Marcus was looking over the price sheet for the show. When he saw Jeff, he stood and presented the chair as a servant might to a king.

"How was your meeting?" Marcus asked.

"Fine," Jeff said. "He invited me to a dinner."

"A dinner?"

"For Sasha," Jeff said.

"Do you even know who that is?"

"A collector?"

Marcus smiled.

"No?"

"Try not to step on too many heads on your way up," Marcus said.

Jeff arrived on time. The restaurant was elegant, with a checkerboard floor and white tablecloths. He felt immediately self-conscious despite being in his best clothes, the same outfit he'd bought for the opening. The hostess asked for the name of the party, and when he said Arsenault, she raised her eyebrows and smiled, asking him to follow her upstairs. She led him to a private dining room, with a table set for twelve, overlooking the main dining room. It was empty. The hostess left him with a menu and returned downstairs. He stood before the table, unsure where to sit. He knew well enough not to take either end, and that he should probably sit with his back to the view of the dining room below, which left him with five seats to choose from. The middle was out—those would be occupied by people of secondary importance to the ones on the ends. This left the corners or the second seat in. The corners allowed for sotto voce conversations with the important people on the end, which made them more valuable than the second seat in. Guessing that Francis would sit at the end farthest from the entrance—as he had in his own home, leaving Alison in the seat closest to the kitchen—Jeff placed himself in the second seat from the end, his back to the view.

Try not to step on too many heads on your way up. He'd shared Marcus's words with Chloe. She supposed that Marcus was jealous of the attention Jeff was getting. She advised him not to worry about the others, only about himself. And if everything went upside down, who cared, he could get a job somewhere else. She wasn't going anywhere.

A waiter came and asked if he wanted a drink. He didn't know what the protocol was, whether there would be alcohol or it would be more of a working dinner, and so he ordered an iced tea. The menu he'd been handed turned out to be customized. Dinner in honor of Alex Post, the artist whose show was currently up at the gallery, the one who had looked like a construction worker. No mention of Sasha. The date and time printed on the menu reassured Jeff that he was indeed where he was supposed to be.

Ten minutes later, a young woman entered, led by the hostess, who handed her a menu and disappeared back downstairs, leaving her standing at the end of the table. She was tall, very thin, not much older than Jeff. But she came from a different universe. She looked like she could have been a runway model but was doing everything she could to dispel notions of conventional beauty, yet without quite making herself ugly. She wore makeup, mascara and blush, hastily applied. Her hair was dyed a number of colors, pulled tight into a bun with a chopstick through it. She wore a thrift-store cardigan over what looked like a very expensive champagne slip dress. She didn't hesitate in choosing a seat, but went around to the other side of the table and installed herself on the corner, which, according to Jeff's calculations, would put her at the right hand of Francis. She hung a bag over the back of her chair and sat. Her nails were short and her hands stained with pigment.

Jeff introduced himself. She smiled a pro forma smile and said her name was Astrid. She spoke with an unidentifiable accent, Eastern European, though later that evening it would slip into a pseudo–British English, peppered with American colloquialisms. He asked her if she knew when everyone else was going to arrive. She shrugged, clearly not interested in conversation. The waiter appeared and asked if she wanted a drink. She ordered something Jeff had never heard of, on the rocks. He asked her if she was an artist, and she said yes, with a little smile in the corner of her mouth that said she knew he wasn't.

Jeff studied the menu but couldn't make much sense of it. Shanghai little dragon? Drunken fish? Gambler's duck? Lily bulb with mountain yam?

The rest of the party arrived then, Alex Post in his coveralls, Francis in a blue linen suit with no tie, and a few men and women in their forties or fifties, looking as though they had through wealth escaped into a world without consequences. Funky eyeglasses, a striped jacket, and one woman's cape made it clear to anyone who saw them that they were nonconformists, people of taste, art-world cognoscenti.

Francis sat where Jeff had expected him to, and as he sat, he greeted Astrid in a friendly but not effusive manner. Jeff saw what the others didn't, or didn't care to. Francis's hand landing on Astrid's, giving it a squeeze.

She was beautiful in an alien way, and her youth must have appealed to Francis. It held no sway over Jeff, who could only imagine her crawling across the bed like a spider, all arms and legs.

More drinks were ordered. Jeff got himself a gin and tonic this time. He observed the conversations quietly, trying to sort out who was who and making sure that his mouth wasn't hanging open.

It was a long time before Francis acknowledged him, and then only to absentmindedly introduce Jeff as someone new to the gallery, no job title.

Food arrived. Jeff was famished. He ate everything put in front of him, careful not to outpace the other guests. Astrid didn't touch her food but instead waxed philosophical at Francis and two of the collectors. She was going on and on about process and surfaces and the pitfalls of work that was little more than decorative. Once Jeff sorted out what she was trying to say, he noticed that she talked in circles, and the men listened, letting her go on and on while they admired her. She had been granted entry into this world for the most superficial reasons and was playing the role of someone of substance. As soon as he thought this, he checked himself. What did he know? Maybe she was a brilliant artist. Maybe she wasn't even Francis's mistress. In those days he questioned his judgment whenever it veered toward contempt.

The man to his right appeared to be a collector. He acted as though he was being wooed by Francis, then, when that didn't seem to work, tried to ingratiate himself with him. It was obvious he had a lot of money, he casually dropped the insane numbers he'd spent on blue-chip work, but Francis didn't want to talk money at that hour, or was playing hard to get. The collector blazed with insecurity, trying to convert his wealth into status, or cachet, or—it saddened Jeff to think of it—friendship.

At the other end of the table, Alex Post was already several drinks in, exchanging profound questions and outrageous statements with his fellow artist, the man in the striped jacket. They put on a bit of theater, Jeff thought, in exchange for meals and drinks and the sale of their work. It didn't seem to bother them.

To Jeff's left sat the woman with the cape. She remained quiet. Initially Jeff worried that she wasn't having a good time, because she didn't speak, but when he looked more closely, he detected a faint and enduring look of amusement in her eyes. He introduced himself, and they struck up a conversation, a tête-à-tête refuge from the bustling table.

He asked her if she knew Sasha.

She said that besides her husband, he was her favorite of all the FAFA artists.

"I mean, look at him. The coveralls alone," she said, gesturing at Alex Post.

Jeff nodded to mask his confusion. Later that evening Chloe would explain to him that Sasha was a common Eastern European nickname for Alexander.

The woman asked whether he'd noticed any changes in Francis. He told her he hadn't been working for him that long, then asked what changes she'd meant.

He'd always been shady in his business dealings, she said, robbing Peter to pay Paul, as they say, but now he was, in her words, openly fucking over his own artists. For one thing, he'd demanded new work from her husband, who was in a delicate

phase, an incubatory phase, and when her husband failed to provide the new work, he stole unfinished work from the studio,
faked her husband's signature, and sold it. Her husband didn't
say a thing. How could he? The checks were in the bank. He was
being beaten down, her husband was, by Francis, sucked dry too,
and soon there would be nothing left.

Jeff looked to the artist in the striped jacket on the other side
of the table. Was he the husband? He was laughing at something
Alex Post had said, looking happy and full of life.

"Cocaine," said the woman, following Jeff's eyes. "Hell of a
drug."

Jeff wondered why Francis had invited him. He wasn't meeting
collectors or catering to the whims of eccentric artists. Rather,
he was watching a bunch of old people party and absorbing the
gripes of a blocked artist's wife. He looked to Astrid in the corner,
tried to gauge her face. She was no longer monologuing, but
smiling vacantly and twitching or wincing, Jeff couldn't be sure.
Francis wore a devilish grin. His hand was under the table.

"I have to hand it to him," said the artist's wife, "he's got
chutzpah. Never asks anyone's permission. An unstoppable object in search of an immovable mass. When he broke his ribs,
we dropped off a care package, a little token, and you wouldn't
believe how happy Alison was to see us. She asked us to take him
with us. A joke, but you just know she meant it. I didn't get to
see any of the madness firsthand. He was upstairs zonked out on
Vicodin, with strict orders not to let anyone ever, ever, ever see
him asleep.

"Do you think he knows I'm talking about him right now?"
she asked.

Jeff looked toward Francis, who was already looking in his direction. He gave Jeff a blank look, an uninterpretable look, then
smiled and asked if he was having a good time.

41

"I said yes, of course I said yes, but honestly I had no idea what kind of time I was having. My head was spinning from the whole thing, from Astrid, from the woman next to me, from the artists, the collectors, from being in that fancy restaurant in the first place. Not to mention the drinks. I tried to take it easy, but they just kept coming. My technique in those days, and it wasn't a bad one, was to avoid opening my mouth at all when I was drunk. In vino veritas. Don't say anything, don't say anything stupid."

"Wise."

"Not exactly employing it now," he said, raising his glass. "But I doubt I'll ever see you again."

"Give it another couple of decades," I said.

A chuckle from him, but nothing in his eyes to signal that he hadn't meant it seriously. It felt like a curtain had been pulled back, then let fall again.

"You've kept all this to yourself for a long time," I said, breaking the silence.

He nodded.

"And now you've chosen to tell me."

"As I said, seeing you . . . got the ball rolling." He searched for the right words. "Look, we're not getting any younger. That surgery I mentioned. I found myself in a forest dark and all that. Dante."

"Right," I said.

"And then there you were. Kismet."

I must have looked skeptical because he continued.

"I suppose I've been feeling a pressure to share my story with another soul for a while now." He put his hands together, smiled grimly. "Who better than someone who was there at the beginning?"

"You said that before. Only I'm not sure why it matters."

"You knew me then. That I had a good heart."

Knew him? It would have been generous to call us acquaintances. I felt like I was being pressed to testify to something I hadn't actually witnessed.

"At the very least," he said, "I know that you won't convert it into something that can be held over me."

"I'm not planning to blackmail you, if that's what you mean."

"People blackmail each other every day. We're all keepers of each other's secrets."

Blackmail was one thing, secrets were another. He knew I was a writer. I was starting to think that that was the point, or had become the point. The self-portrait.

"I can't make any guarantees," I said.

"Stick with me here."

There it was again, that phrase. His insistence on it reminded me of a telemarketer's assurances that their call is purely informational—while behind every phrase, every detail, lurks the specter of a sales pitch.

"That dinner was a turning point for me," Jeff said, "because until then I had been accumulating my own data, not coming to any conclusions, holding off on passing judgment. But when that woman spoke to me, it was as if she were giving form to my cloudy, nascent thoughts. She put into words for me what was plainly obvious but which I had not ventured to declare, even to myself. Francis was an asshole."

"And you gave him new life."

"That I did," Jeff said, tossing back the rest of his drink.

42

That weekend Chloe picked up Jeff in her little BMW and took him to check out the progress on the Mandeville house.

The site was protected by a green-fabric-covered chain-link construction fence, but the gate had been chained loosely enough that they were able to slide through. On the other side, Chloe stopped short, looking up at the massive steel beam and wood framing.

"All I can think about is the house that used to be here."

"You miss it?"

The old house had been cozy, she said, with invisible paths grooved through it from all their years of living there. It had been a home, a real home. Unlike this behemoth, which was little more than an absurd showpiece for her father and blank canvas for her mother.

They entered through a large opening into what would one day be the foyer. Jeff could see through the whole structure to the hillside at the back of the lot.

"It just keeps going," he said.

"You have no idea." She led him across the plywood subfloor to a large rectangular hole, where a set of stairs led down into the basement, not a California basement, but a basement as large as the footprint of the entire house, a basement with what must have been ten-foot ceilings. Light shone down from airshafts at the perimeter, reflecting off hundreds of linear feet of cut pine, lending everything a golden-yellow cast.

"Jesus," he said, his voice echoing off the concrete outer walls.

"My dad's all about the square footage."

Chloe led him along what would become the hallway, past what would become the laundry room, the maid's room, and so on. As Chloe rattled off the rooms, he was struck by a kind of horizontal vertigo, a sense that he was no longer in the same house, on the same street, but in a generic, undefined space, far from anywhere.

They came to a large chamber at the end of the hall.

"This is going to be a movie theater."

Chloe's melancholy over the loss of her childhood home had evaporated, replaced with an emergent enthusiasm. Jeff tried to look impressed, but his thoughts, as usual, were with Francis.

"If you had to describe your dad," he asked, "like what kind of person he is, how would you describe him?"

He didn't expect much perspective—we don't get perspective on our own families until very late, if ever—but was hoping that she might shed some light on Francis's being-in-the-world.

Chloe asked why he'd brought it up.

He told her about the artist's wife, and how critical of Francis she'd been.

She shrugged it off. "The lady sounds bitter," she said.

He mentioned the accusation that Francis had stolen unfinished work from the studio and forged the artist's signature.

Chloe laughed. She agreed that it was "a dick move" but said that she wasn't surprised in the least.

What about the way he treated his employees, Jeff pointed out, snapping at them and berating them for seemingly no reason?

"He's a shark," she said. "They knew what they were getting into."

Everything he threw in her direction was deflected, but instead of frustrating him, it calmed him.

Only later would he recognize how distracted he'd been by her beauty, by her presence, by the chemicals flowing through his veins as they embraced in the subterranean would-be theater's half-light.

Only later, too, would he learn that the offenses he'd enumerated were of no import to Chloe, not because she felt one way or another about them, but because they didn't affect her personally.

43

Thus Jeff drifted toward Chloe's point of view, that her father was a character, a bit rough around the edges, but not a bad guy, necessarily, and that the artist's wife had been venting, giving voice to what must have been sour grapes. This was no doubt aided by the positive reinforcement he was getting from Francis, who had pulled him off the front desk and into Fiona's office, to work on digitizing the gallery, bringing it into the twenty-first century. Francis had pegged Jeff as a computer whiz, and Jeff did little to disabuse him of that notion. His newly acquired knowledge of Microsoft Excel had catapulted him to "database wizard" status, and he set about making himself indispensable.

Fiona—who, per Marcus, knew "where the bodies were buried"—welcomed Jeff into her registrar's world, where, he discovered, she was already well on the way to digitizing the gallery's data. A peculiarity in her character made her reluctant to claim credit for the work. She seemed to prefer the perverse joy of being the only one, save Jeff, who knew that she was the motive force behind these digital renovations. Whether this was from a sense of modesty or knowing better than to stick her head up for Francis to whack, Jeff couldn't tell.

Meanwhile, Francis yelled at Marcus and Andrea whenever he had the chance. Now that Jeff was upstairs, he could hear the content of the yelling. Some of it sounded familiar, a more expletive-filled, splenetic version of the speech Francis had given Jeff. His tirades were usually provoked by a piece of unexpected news. If said news was printed in an art-world publication, and Francis hadn't already heard about it, he could rant for a solid ten minutes about the incompetence of his employees. Marcus and Andrea would do their fair share of salaaming, and Francis, depleted, would return to his office, shutting the door behind him. Often they wouldn't even know what he'd gotten riled up about until well afterward.

During these episodes, Fiona would become very quiet, as if by making any noise she might attract Francis's attention and become the target of his ire. Jeff never heard Francis yell at Fiona.

This was no doubt because of the information she kept under digital and physical lock and key. The more Jeff saw of it, the more he became convinced that the gallery was all but a criminal enterprise. Money sloshed around via wire, and artworks of dubious provenance moved from collector to collector trailed by 1031 like-kind exchange tax forms, deferring taxes even as the work appreciated, or so Jeff understood, when Fiona explained it.

He saw the allegedly unfinished work Francis had pilfered from the artist's studio, with the allegedly forged signature, sold to a collector, shipped straight to a warehouse. And other work, some of which they didn't have photos of, and which lay outside what the gallery would show, a group of four Picasso works on paper, a Dürer, a Matisse, moving from hand to hand in an artworld version of musical chairs.

One afternoon, Jeff was scanning photographs into the computer when he saw Astrid in the upstairs hallway, carrying a small portfolio box. He greeted her as an old friend, and she returned his greeting as coolly as expected. In her unidentifiable accent, she said she was dropping off a batch of transparencies for Francis to look over. New work. He wasn't in the office, Jeff said. Astrid set the portfolio box on the desk and carefully removed from it a smaller archival-type box, about four by five inches. She delivered it to Jeff with both hands. She might as well have been handing over her child. He told her he would make sure Francis got them. She gathered her portfolio and looked at him blankly. He assured her a second time that Francis would get the transparencies the moment he walked into the office. She gave a curt nod and left. When she turned, her wide-necked sweater slid to the side, revealing a scarlet bra strap.

He looked at the transparencies as soon as she was downstairs. The work consisted of a series of six square paintings, large, seventy-two inches by seventy-two inches, each of which was a nude portrait of a thin woman, posed so that her form filled almost the whole canvas. He respected the effort, and the scale, but the works, in transparency form at least, left him cold. Not in technique—Astrid could paint—but in something else, Jeff wasn't sure how to express it. Clarity of vision. Or impetus. Yes, that was it, he couldn't figure out the impetus behind the paintings, other than to show off Astrid's facility for painting.

He delivered the box to Francis's desk, staring at the nimbus painting on the wall for a moment, the absence of the man. He hadn't been in there alone before, hadn't had a reason or excuse, and now he struggled to resist the urge to snoop. What if he were to pull open one of Francis's desk drawers? What would he find inside? He decided to try one, only one. Pretending (for nobody) that he was making sure the portfolio box was in the right place, he reached down below the surface of the desk and pulled the handle. It was locked.

44

A few days later, Francis called Jeff into his office. Cooped up with Fiona, Jeff hadn't noticed Francis's arrival. He'd been in Manhattan for a few days, checking in on his gallery there. Astrid's transparencies were stacked on the box they'd come in, at one end of Francis's desk. Jeff glanced at them, and Francis followed his eyes.

"She said she dropped them off with you. Did you get a chance to look at them?"

Jeff shook his head. He knew better than to step into that mess.

"Take a look," Francis said. "I'd love to hear your thoughts."

Jeff protested—he didn't have much of an eye, he told Francis.

"An eye? Bullshit. The only thing you need is the courage of your convictions."

"But everyone talks about your eye. *You* talk about your eye."

"Only because it would be impolite to talk about my balls," Francis said. "It's art. I could take anything and pump it up or tear it down."

Jeff reached for the transparencies. "You want me to pump it up or tear it down?" he asked.

"Just tell me what you think. Does she have it or not?"

Jeff examined the images again, holding the slides up to the light coming through the window. "The bodies are almost geometric," he said, "and seem confined in the square of the canvas like they're in a glass cube. It's claustrophobic. But the skin textures are really complex, they create an opening, something to look at, so that you're escaping the claustrophobia through them—"

Francis was next to him, looking through the same transparency.

"Remind me to have you write catalogue copy," he said.

"For Astrid?"

Francis laughed once, almost a cough. "No, no, no. This is student work. Skinny girl Jenny Savilles."

Another name Jeff didn't know.

"Astrid can paint," Francis said, "but her work is not yet her own, if you catch my drift."

This was what Jeff had sensed the first time he looked at them. He had thought of it as a question of impetus and motivation rather than originality. Nevertheless, he felt buoyed by the idea that he had perceived something in a work of art that fell in line with Francis's far more educated and experienced view. It was the first inkling that he too might develop an eye, a real eye, not a euphemism for balls, for the ability to push his opinion regardless of the underlying material, but an actual aesthetic sense. Which Francis himself did possess, his self-deprecating comments and domineering tactics aside.

Francis gathered the transparencies and put them back in the box. Replacing the cover, he sighed, and it seemed to Jeff that he was already steeling himself to face Astrid and an inevitably dull and treacherous conversation about her work.

But he hadn't been called into the office to look at Astrid's work. Francis wanted Jeff to accompany him to Sotheby's, down the block, to check on a painting by one of his artists that was coming up for auction. He wanted to know the presale estimate and the prospect for the sale. Did they have any buyers lined up already, et cetera. Jeff asked him how he felt about collectors turning around and auctioning works they bought from his gallery.

Francis declared that he would never sell to that collector again. That said, from time to time, one needed to prime the pump to keep the secondary market moving. The artist had a show coming up in the spring, and a good result at the fall auctions could boost both values and interest.

"What if the work doesn't sell?" Jeff asked.

Francis took a beat to figure out how to put it. "There are two kinds of idiot in this world, Jeff. Those who hope for the best, and those who prepare for the worst. I am neither."

"You know it's going to sell?"

"I like to eliminate uncertainty, let's put it that way."

Jeff thought about this all the way to Sotheby's. He supposed it to mean that Francis had a buyer on his payroll, someone who could make sure the painting was bid up to a certain level, bolstering the artist's secondary market. But what if that buyer won? Would Francis openly buy back a work by one of his artists? Perhaps he had enlisted one of his collectors. This struck Jeff as a form of insider trading, but he wasn't sure who the victims were. If the market said the work was worth five million, then it was worth five million. Collectors who then bought work at inflated prices in the spring were likely to want to keep those prices up and would participate in doing so. The only situation in which real fraud would occur, real fraud as opposed to the system as a whole, which struck Jeff as inherently fraudulent, was one in which a market was created out of thin air and then abandoned, with some taking profits and others left holding the bag, as it were. But Francis wouldn't do that—he was playing the long game.

It wasn't lost on Jeff that they were walking the same sidewalk he'd once followed Francis down clandestinely. His circumstances were so transformed that he could hardly bring to mind the feverish intensity he'd felt at the sight of Francis walking on his own, dry, alive. It seemed an impossibly long time ago, though it wasn't, as if a narrow but impassable chasm kept magnifying its impassability by getting deeper and deeper. Still, something of it remained with him, unresolved. He would always, in the context of Francis, remember that none of this would be happening without his having intervened that morning on the beach. What he didn't know, and couldn't decide, was where or when or how he might lay claim to that action. For now, he would watch the repercussions unfold, or rather, participate in them, following the new course of his life, charted by an accidental encounter with someone else's mortality.

Or, he thought, if he possessed the strength to keep his secret forever, he might be able to enjoy the life into which he'd serendipitously slipped, not as reward—he refused to see it in those terms, that way corrosion lay—but as a chain of circumstances arising from his decision—how easy it was to recast it as a decision now, rather than what he'd felt forced to do—his noble decision to come to the aid of a stranger in distress.

Could he set it all aside, the trauma, the confusion, the echoes of his heartbreak over G, and commit to this life? Cling to the old life preserver of *everything happens for a reason*? Walking down the street toward Sotheby's, with the shadow of his past tracing the same route, he thought it might be possible.

The auction house's imposing front desk was manned by staffers in their twenties wearing black suits. They knew Francis by sight. He and Jeff walked straight to the offices. The large space had a surprisingly low ceiling. People tapped away in cubicles, while beyond, others stood at a long table, perusing what looked to be layouts for catalogues. Francis found who he was looking for, a thirtysomething woman with a glimmer of the hunt in her eye, someone who enjoyed a good battle, Jeff sensed, and they made their way into a gallery where works were being hung for a preview event in a week's time.

Francis didn't introduce anyone to Jeff, nor did anyone acknowledge him other than with a perfunctory closed-mouth smile. Through the doorway, Jeff noticed a man making his way down the length of the offices, led by a senior Sotheby's employee in a neat black suit. It took him a moment to realize who the figure was. Francis recognized him at the same moment, told Jeff to wait there, and marched across the offices, arm outstretched, to shake hands with Mick Jagger.

The woman followed Francis, and Jeff was left alone in the small gallery filled with a variety of paintings, some still wrapped, some hanging, some leaning against the wall. He found himself, yet again, searching for something in the work to stimulate something inside him. Eye or no eye, he should have an opinion about these pieces, shouldn't he? He found the painting by Francis's artist, a thickly impastoed palette knife production in dark tones that could have just as easily been a patch of dirt in a field somewhere, or a compost pile. The estimate had not yet been posted.

A large painting across the room caught his eye, leaning against the wall, a diptych. He was drawn in not only by its monumental scale but also by its complexity, its energy, its dynamics, and its seemingly unresolved and unresolvable nature. He didn't look at it so much as watch it. He let his eyes move across the surface, taking in the strokes of dark brown, blue, yellow, orange, lavender, and white; the blobs, the drips, the forceful gestures, the accidents, the way the seam between the two panels bisected the floating cloud, or blob, or explosion, so that it looked as if the left side and right side were painted at different times, from different vantage points, the lines not quite connecting, the right side magnified and shifted up a foot. The canvases almost connected, and, in distribution of color and gesture, the overall image was almost symmetrical, so that if he thought about it—which he did not until later, much later—part of the painting's overall dynamic mimicked what happens when our eyes cross or are affected by different lenses or are in some way uncoupled from each other. Double vision, a parallax view, an image refusing to resolve into a single perspective. He would look back on this moment many times and feel the same fluttering in his chest he felt upon first encountering this work, and no matter how he tried to reduce his response to logic or reason he would always fail. Only after he'd stood there for who knew how long did he think to read the label to find out who had made the painting. Joan Mitchell. Painted in 1986. Both the plainness of the name and the recent date didn't fit, for him, the idea of artistic genius, which was, he had been taught, always foreign and always old. The estimate seemed too low for such a profound work, at least compared to the numbers he'd come in contact with while working at FAFA, though when he thought about it in the context of real-world funds, the low estimate comprised ten years of his earnings. And yet even while that seemed ridiculous, it still seemed to him too low. In the distance between these values he felt himself recalibrating. And in the field of energy created by the painting, he felt intimations of an eye of his own.

Francis entered the gallery, vibrating with energy after his encounter with Mick Jagger. He sidled up next to Jeff, who hadn't taken his eyes off the painting.

"Woof," Francis said.

45

"He didn't care for it?" I asked.

Jeff nodded. "But it was my first encounter with the sublime in a work of art." Jeff pronounced the word *sublime* with eyes-shut reverence. "I asked him what he didn't like about it, and all he said was 'second-gen AbEx,' which meant nothing to me, but which I assumed, correctly, meant that his woofing had to do with the soft market for the piece. The funny thing is, if I'd had the funds back then, and if I'd gone with my eye, my gut, whatever, I could have sold it later for ten times what I'd have paid. You see, I did have good instincts. I just didn't know it yet."

How quickly he moved from the aesthetic to the mercantile.

"Francis saw it in you," I said.

"If he did, it wasn't through any particular acumen. Francis was incapable of seeing, really seeing, other people. It was both his superpower and his greatest weakness. As a result, he never saw me for me. But what I suppose was different in my case, as opposed to those he treated with undiluted instrumentality, was that when he looked at me, he believed he was looking in a mirror. A back-in-time mirror."

"Do you think his having nearly died brought his mortality to the front of his mind?"

"No question about it. In fact, he pulled me aside once, at the gallery—he had been trying to make a point, and Marcus and Andrea weren't listening sufficiently for him—he pulled me aside to tell me how refreshing it was to have someone around who could actually absorb his lessons. As if I were a sponge. But I think he really did see me as a sponge, as the second-best thing to uploading his consciousness into a giant computer. Which he would have done if he could have. Silicon immortality, it was a side interest of his. This was before anyone talked about it outside of science fiction novels. Francis couldn't stand the idea that everything in his head—his opinions, his feelings, his memories—would one day disappear."

"Couldn't have helped that he was surrounded by artists," I said.

Jeff went to sip his drink, forgetting it was empty.

"I guess he needed an outlet," he said.

"Don't we all."

46

At the Sunday dinners, Francis treated Jeff more and more like a confidant. One night they had a few more drinks than usual, and while Chloe and her mother were in the kitchen, Francis invited Jeff to come sit with him in the front room and smoke Cubans. He wanted to talk. This was during a period when, at the gallery, Marcus was trying to assert himself more, brandishing his squash racquet and pulling rank on Jeff whenever he could. Francis had somehow gotten wind of this and wasn't happy about it, but not because of Marcus's behavior. He wasn't happy because Jeff wasn't standing up for himself.

"You should go after what you want," he said. "Go after *everything* you want. That's what youth is for, Jeff. You're a good kid, I see that, I saw that the first day I met you. But you must understand that there is no good or bad, only advantageous and its opposite."

Jeff listened, concerned mainly with appearing as though he was taking in Francis's advice when the vehemence of the way the words were delivered made him want to turn away. His eyes watered.

"There's no reason to be good, Jeff. I can tell you this honestly. No reason."

He seemed lost in thought for a moment, and when he resumed, it was in a calmer but more intense register.

"I died once," he said. "Actually, truly died. They had to bring me back."

"Oh my God," Jeff said.

"And you know what was on the other side?"

"No."

"Nothing."

"Oh."

"No white light, no grandparents, no St. Peter, no Satan. Just a blank. Oblivion. I was swimming." He looked into Jeff's eyes with fierce intensity. "Just chugging along. I've never been particularly fast. I always sort of shoved my way through the water. Not unlike how I move through life." He laughed. "And the next thing I know, I'm on the sand, coughing up water. Probably what a baby feels like when it's born. I'm on the fucking sand and the paramedics are there, strapping me up, taking me to the hospital. Which is full of doctors who have no idea what happened other than my heart stopped. It would have been nice to know why, right? These two"—he pointed toward the kitchen—"won't let me go in the water again."

Jeff's palms were slick with sweat. His eyes stung from the cigar smoke. Francis looked at him in silence, drew on his cigar, the cherry shining brightly in the dim room. Was he waiting for Jeff to react, to declare that he had been there, that he had been the one to save him, or was he only watching to make sure his message was sinking in? Jeff copied Francis, took a drag from his cigar, and his head started spinning.

"That could have been it for me," Francis said. "If someone hadn't been there . . ."

Jeff excused himself to use the bathroom, where he promptly threw up his dinner.

Chloe arrived immediately with a cup of water, admonishing her father for getting her boyfriend sick. Francis cackled in the other room, saying the blame lay entirely with Jeff, he was a big boy, Francis hadn't forced anything on him. Alison scolded him from the kitchen, Francis countered. Jeff lay his head on the toilet seat while Chloe stroked his hair.

47

"Excuse me." Saskia from the reception desk materialized in front of us. "Your flight has been cleared, but there is the matter of gathering a new crew. So you will be flying this evening, but please be patient with us."

We thanked her, and she went in search of other refugees from our flight.

The sun had disappeared over the horizon. It was almost completely dark outside. The planes and their service vehicles were lit up, but in the dark parts of the view, the windows had been taken over by our reflections.

"Do you think it was possible that Francis knew?"

"Of course it was possible, anything is possible. At the time, in moments of anxiety and paranoia, I was sure he knew. Why else would he pay me so much attention? And then I'd talk myself down. I reminded myself that I was dating his daughter, that I reminded him of himself, that I was like the son he'd never had, and so on. It was a function of my self-esteem, I decided. If I believed myself worthy of Francis's attention, then of course he didn't remember me from the beach. If I thought myself unworthy, I could find no other reason for him to keep me close."

"What do you think now?"

"I think that some part of him might have known then, but strictly subconsciously."

"Resulting in a bias toward you?"

"Correct."

"But you didn't press him on it? Ask about who rescued him?"

Jeff shook his head. "I didn't dare. We'd only just achieved a kind of equilibrium, a family dynamic, I guess you could say. I'd never had it growing up, so it was hard to recognize, also in general it's hard to know when things are going well, it's like your health, you take it for granted to the degree that it becomes invisible to you. Nevertheless, I knew that were I to reveal my role in Francis's rescue, everything would have come crashing down. I'm sure he would have been grateful, but the way I'd inserted myself into his life, which I would contend was basically accidental, the result of a series of decisions I hadn't fully thought through, would have immediately cast a cloud of mistrust over me.

"I'd had an anxiety attack that night. Even the music that was playing in the background, it was jazz, the same Charlie Parker mix I had played in the gallery, dissolved into chaos, notes falling all over one another, torn out of time. While sitting there on the floor of the Arsenault bathroom, my face on the cool toilet seat, Chloe stroking my hair, my panic receding, I realized that the source of the attack wasn't hearing Francis's account of the rescue, wasn't the prospect of reliving the event that had, as you put it, traumatized me. The source was a dawning fear that as a result of this whole ordeal I had become monstrously deceptive and selfish, on the order of Francis himself, as if he had infected me the moment I had put my mouth to his, and that by some operation of cosmic justice this would be exposed, and that everything around me, everything I had so recently begun, and, without any force of will or malicious intent, had come to treasure, would be stripped from me."

48

Everything was about to be overturned, but not by Jeff, not by his secret or his action or inaction. Not even by his complacence, his comfort, his desire for everything to stay the same. No, life was about to go upside down because of another secret, one Francis was keeping.

One night, Chloe called Jeff, sobbing. She had just been attacked, she said. He asked if she was all right, if she had called the police, if he needed to drive down there right away. Verbally, she said, I was attacked verbally. He asked her who had done it and where and why, and again asked her if she was okay. She said she was not okay, she was miserable and confused and angry. She had been at a party thrown by one of the art MFAs when a woman, an MFA student, pulled her aside. She didn't know this person—she'd seen her around, of course, she was aware of the graduate students, but she had never met her. The student was shaking, on the verge of tears. She said her name was Astrid.

Jeff's stomach dropped. Astrid? He asked her what she looked like. Chloe said it didn't matter, she was pretty, too skinny, about Jeff's age, a few years older, kooky hair.

Away from the main party, tucked into an alcove by the kitchen, Astrid asked Chloe if her last name was indeed Arsenault.

"Yes," Chloe said.

"Your father is Francis Arsenault?"

"Yes," Chloe said.

"He's a bastard," said Astrid. She proceeded to tell her all about how her father had led her along, showing interest in her work, all but telling her he was going to sign her, give her a show, at least put a piece in a group show, or hang her work in the back room. He'd done a studio visit, she said. And she had done everything she could to put everything she had into her new paintings, thinking—no, knowing—the whole time that they would, or at least one would, be hanging in FAFA sometime over the next year.

Astrid was manic, voice shaking. Chloe looked for a way to extricate herself from the situation. She had never been called to task for her father's business decisions, nor should she have been. Astrid started to slur her words, recognized it, and proceeded to overenunciate every phrase.

Chloe looked around for another MFA student to confirm that Astrid had crossed a line, but nobody met her eye. And yet she could feel their gazes, as if some of them knew what was happening, what was going to happen, experiencing the schadenfreude of someone else's career suicide, because even if Chloe wasn't doing anything then, even if she couldn't escape or respond or shut down Astrid, she would without hesitation describe this episode in its entirety to her father.

Her work was supposed to be shown at FAFA, Astrid continued, it was the deal, it was part of the deal, he couldn't pretend it wasn't now, who cared if they never shook on it, if there was nothing on paper, he had promised her, and besides—Astrid became curiously still then, as if to steady her aim before firing a kill shot—he must have known, he couldn't not have known, that if he hadn't been who he was, if he hadn't held the power and the allure and the access, there was no way in a million years she would have fucked him.

On the phone, Chloe sniffled. "How messed up is that?" she asked Jeff.

Jeff asked her if it was possible Astrid was lying, or that someone was pulling a prank. He said this half-heartedly, knowing what he had known since he saw Francis place his hand on Astrid's at Mr. Chow, but a part of him hoped that all this could go away, that he could go back to the time before he picked up the phone to a sobbing Chloe.

If it was a prank, Chloe said, then Astrid was a hell of an actress. She had unleashed the full force of her fury, pain, and frustration at Chloe, without restraint or tempering. She was going to blow everything up, even if she took herself out in the process.

Jeff thought of Astrid's work, the transparencies he'd seen. How could she have believed that she was ready for a show at FAFA? Didn't she realize she'd be torn apart by reviews? Or was she one of those people who had no capacity for self-awareness, someone so sure of her own success that a no was an affront, if only because it ran counter to what should have been obvious to anyone with a functioning pair of eyes, which was that her work was brilliant? She certainly carried that arrogance with her at dinner, and again when she dropped off the transparencies. He was surprised to hear that she'd crumbled so publicly, but then again, those kinds of people were often more fragile than they seemed. Harder, but more brittle.

"You know," Jeff said, "if you keep it to yourself, you could prevent Astrid from having any power over the situation."

"True."

"Otherwise you're playing right into her hands."

Chloe cleared her throat. The line was quiet for a moment. "I wouldn't be able to face my mom. To face my dad or my mom. If I kept it a secret, I mean. At the very least I have to give my dad the opportunity to defend himself, right? What if she did make the whole thing up?"

"Possible," Jeff said.

"Wishful thinking, though."

"You never know," Jeff said.

"But I do."

She returned to the idea of keeping the secret. She wouldn't be able to do it, she was sure. She was incapable of carrying something like that around, something she knew could upend everything, a truth, or a potential truth, that needed, in her opinion, to be out in the world. Like a woodpecker in her mind, tapping at the inside of her skull. She would tell, she had to tell, she would describe the encounter, that was all, nothing about whether she believed it or not.

Jeff asked if she was worried about Francis's reaction. They both knew how he could be when he was angry.

"I can't tell him anything he doesn't know already," she said. "I'm going to tell my mom."

49

Chloe arrived on his doorstep early the next morning looking as though she hadn't slept. She asked Jeff if he would come with her to her parents' house, to talk to her mom. She needed someone to be there, and she knew that it was Jeff's day off. He said it was the least he could do, though he dreaded the scene. Together they took the old Volvo into Santa Monica.

Francis had already left for work. At the curb, Chloe asked Jeff if he would mind waiting in the car. She'd realized she didn't want him to be there when she told her mother, but she wanted him nearby. He tried not to show his relief at being allowed to stay away from the epicenter.

She gathered herself, looked him in the eyes, and said a somewhat formal *thank you.* Then she was across the street and through the front door.

He waited patiently with the windows rolled down, the car off but the radio on, tuned to 91.5 KUSC, the classical station. He couldn't see anything through the front window of the house. Not that Alison and Chloe would necessarily have their conversation in the living room, but the sun had made a mirror of the glass.

A gardener's truck pulled up and parked in front of him, and he watched the gardener bringing the mower out of the back of the truck on little wooden ramps he'd connected to the tailgate. He could smell the gasoline and the dry yard trimmings. The gardener started the mower, and Jeff rolled up his windows.

He tried to imagine what was going on inside the house. Would Alison fly into a rage? Would she pick up the phone and call Francis immediately, to see whether he would confirm or deny what Astrid had said? He couldn't quite picture it, but to be fair, he'd never seen her presented with devastating news.

The gardener and his coworker finished their rounds, reloaded the truck, and drove off. Jeff lowered the windows again. He started to worry that Chloe had forgotten about him out there, but he knew he couldn't just drive off. Knocking on the door was the obvious solution, and yet he couldn't do it. Invading her privacy would be as bad as disappearing on her. But he couldn't just sit there all day, could he?

For Chloe he would. He leaned his seat back and closed his eyes.

He awoke to the sound of her opening the passenger door. She got in, and he could see by the way she held herself that she wasn't as agitated as she'd been when they arrived. Her eyes were puffy still, and her hair a mess, but she was no longer in a panic. He put his hand on her leg and she put her hand over it. He asked her how it went.

"She tried to make it about me," Chloe said.

After Chloe related the story of Astrid's unhinged confrontation, Alison acted as if the primary injury was to Chloe. As if what had happened was unconnected to herself. She made tea, and asked Chloe if Astrid had hit her or otherwise attacked her physically. She asked Chloe if she felt unsafe at school.

Chloe was incredulous, but this made sense to Jeff. The Alison he knew, the one who made a living feathering other people's nests, was a caretaker.

Chloe had had to repeat herself to her mother, to bring the subject back around to her father and his infidelity. Her mother said that it was between herself and Francis. Frustrated by her mother's equanimity, Chloe asked her if she wasn't angry or hurt or confused by what had happened. Why wasn't she showing Chloe her emotions? They were both adults, after all.

Her mother replied that Chloe had been subjected to enough already.

Chloe asked if her father had done this before. Her mother repeated that some things were better kept between her and Francis.

This was followed by a stilted conversation about Chloe's coursework.

Then just before Chloe left, her mother said that she was right. She was an adult, and so she would level with her. Her father had broken promises in the past, and she wasn't surprised to see it happening again, especially now, considering the Porsche and all that nonsense. It was both expected and unexpected. Her heart hurt, she wouldn't deny it. But whatever she'd been subjected to paled before the fact that Francis had—even if by accident, even if by proximity—roped Chloe into this mess.

For that she couldn't forgive him.

50

Chloe decided to stay with Jeff for a little while. She wanted to be closer to her parents' house if her mother needed her. She was also avoiding USC and any possible encounter with Astrid. She spoke to her mother on the phone every day but didn't share updates with Jeff. No more disclosures would leak beyond the newly reinforced mother-daughter connection.

At work, Jeff figured that his best course of action was to show up and do the job, stay out of it. The official story was that Francis had had to skip off to New York, to broker a private sale. (When Jeff mentioned this to Chloe, she told him it was bullshit. If her mom had been home alone, didn't he think she would have been there with her? Her father was definitely still in town, hunkered down, trying to save the marriage. Francis had gone all in. *Look*, he was no doubt saying, *I have dropped everything for you.* After a sufficient period of penitence, he must have figured, Alison would absorb the blow and let him back in.)

Without Francis around, the office was curiously calm. None of his personal chaos had infected the gallery, unless you counted a bit of graffiti painted on the front glass one night, *bunko*, in large cursive script, which could have just as easily been the work of a random vandal, someone protesting the excesses of the art world or Beverly Hills in general. After a brief debate as to whether the graffiti constituted an artwork in and of itself, it was cleaned up, none of the gallery's employees given any reason to think it had anything to do with Francis, at least not in the context of an affair.

Marcus and Andrea made their sales, Fiona did whatever she did with all her records, and Jeff continued his mission to digitize everything. There was no yelling, no drama. Everything ran smoother without Francis there. The staff even developed a sense of camaraderie, almost.

Yet Jeff knew that despite how tempting it might be to imagine a gallery this peaceful, nobody there had the vision, the chutzpah, "it," to lead. With this crew, FAFA could only follow, probably drift along without Francis for a year, maybe eighteen months, depending on the attrition rate of artists and employees. They'd put up the shows they'd already scheduled, and sell to collectors who already had their eyes on the artists, until, beyond that, it would, like all businesses built around a cult of personality, fade into a shadow of its former self.

51

One morning Jeff arrived to a note on his desk. Francis was back. He was in his office already, and he wanted to see Jeff right away.

Jeff walked down the hall, not knowing what to expect.

Francis wore the face of a man who had been begging, every morning, for another day's stay of execution. Jeff had been correct about Alison's inflicting as much pain as she could. He wondered what had shifted to bring him back to work. Had she begun to let up, to forgive him?

"Come in," he said, "and shut the door."

Jeff sat, waiting, not knowing what he should say or how he should behave.

"As you may know," Francis said.

Jeff nodded.

"I've made a bit of a mess. Nothing terminal."

That was one way to put it, Jeff thought.

"I love my wife," Francis said. "I love her deeply. I wouldn't be the man I am without her." He shifted in his chair. "That said, were she to leave me, as she has the right to, not to mention the reason, I could bear the absence of her affections."

This seemed a strange way to frame the situation.

"However," Francis said, pausing after the word, "the deprivation of filial love I cannot bear."

It was clear that Francis had thought about what he was going to say ahead of time and that he had been turning that phrase over in his mind, editing it, revising it, compressing it for greatest impact. But to Jeff it sounded abstract to the point of near incoherence. He didn't say anything.

"Chloe," Francis clarified.

"Right," Jeff said.

"I haven't lost her, have I?"

Jeff felt it wasn't his place to speak for Chloe, but Francis's penetrating glare demanded an answer.

"I don't think so," Jeff said.

"What you *think* doesn't matter," Francis said. "Alison is on the phone with her every day, God knows what they're talking about. We're going to work it out, as far as I can tell, but I can't tolerate Alison poisoning Chloe against me, if that's what's happening on those calls, and why shouldn't it be? I need to know, definitively. I need you to talk to Chloe and find out where she stands on all of this. Can you do that for me?"

Jeff said he would.

Perceiving that he had found an ally, Francis spoke about his situation more freely.

"Alison blames me for drawing Chloe into this. She has used the word *unforgivable*. And she has forgiven a lot in the past, I don't need to get into that. She won't listen to reason, Jeff. I didn't involve Chloe. It was a pure accident of fate that that little see-you-next-Tuesday Astrid happened to be getting her MFA at USC—I didn't seek her out for that, I wasn't trolling the campus, when I met her I thought she was older, you've seen the way she comports herself. And she is older, in my defense, the way Alison goes on you'd think I'd been fucking an undergraduate. In any case, once Astrid and I had established relations, I understood that they might cross paths, so we were exceptionally discreet about our . . . connection."

Jeff remembered Francis waiting for the elevators at the hotel, lingerie bag in hand.

"Discreet enough. Did you suspect anything at the Alex Post dinner?"

"I did wonder."

Francis looked surprised, then collected himself. "But Chloe wasn't there, was she? Nor was anyone who was likely to tell her, other than you, of course, but you weren't going to fuck yourself in the ass, were you?"

Jeff shook his head.

"No, you know when to keep your mouth shut," Francis said. Something in his eyes might have hinted at a deeper significance there, if only for a moment, but Francis quickly returned to the subject at hand. "As far as I was concerned, despite their potential geographical overlap, Chloe and Astrid occupied distinct, hermetically sealed spheres. One always has to expect leakage with these sorts of things—you can't prevent it. I've gotten in trouble before, but at no point did I think Chloe would be involved. I should have been more careful, I know that now, had I thought anything like this might happen, I would have been a thousand times more careful. But how could I have predicted Astrid's reaction to my not falling all over myself at the sight of her admittedly capable but ultimately shitty paintings? I didn't tell her no, by the way, if I had given her a definitive no, I might be able to understand her reaction a little bit better. I gave her a *not now*, a *not yet*, an *I see potential here*, a *keep going*. But she exploded.

"You know what she said? *I see what this is really about.* Those were her words. As if I were stringing her along, which, I should be crystal clear, I was not. I would have shown her work, eventually. I would have. She would have gotten there, eventually, and I would have shown her work, even if things between us had already ended. I would have."

He repeated it, not as if trying to convince Jeff but himself.

"One sniff of rejection and that petulant little bitch blew the whole thing up. She decided it would be a good idea to approach my daughter? That is not the behavior of a stable person. How has she gotten this far in life? When I told her I wasn't going to hang those paintings, she left in a huff, and I thought she would cool down, I thought she was having an emotional moment and would loop back to talk to me later, but instead she got plastered at a party and imploded her career by making what should have been strictly professional, personal."

Strictly professional. Jeff had to restrain a laugh. Francis was dead serious. In his mind, he and Astrid had been playing by a well-established set of rules. But Astrid had misunderstood, or, frustrated, flipped the table, and she, not the dealer who had dangled a show in front of her in exchange for some pillow time, was to blame.

In the path of this firehose of self-justification, Jeff found himself looking at things from Astrid's perspective. Even if her behavior had been reprehensible and her methods wackadoodle, Jeff thought, her grievance was legitimate.

52

"So Francis thought you were going to work on his behalf, Chloe assumed you were on her side, and your thoughts were with Astrid?"

"It was complicated," Jeff said. "My head was spinning. Francis had taken me under his wing. And I knew about the affair already—it had already been incorporated into the portrait of the man I carried around in my head, returning, always returning, to the fact that none of this would have been happening if it weren't for me. I would have preferred to erase that fact, to deal with everything at face value, but there was no excising it from my thinking, only tolerating its presence, or, I should say, its consistent reappearance.

"But you're right, I had to ask myself whose side I was on, and it came down to this: I wanted to be on everyone's side. Or neutral. Switzerland. It was how I thought of myself, as someone who is good and forgives and doesn't hold grudges and so on. But I couldn't ignore Chloe's pain, and so, despite Francis having been very generous with me, my alignment naturally tilted toward her and, by extension, toward Alison.

"Nevertheless, Francis saw me as an ally, or, at the very least, a go-between, a connection to Chloe, who was consistently refusing to take his calls. For her part, she didn't care for the arrangement, I couldn't blame her, and she wouldn't talk about Francis with me at all. I promised him that progress was being made."

"You lied to him?"

Jeff put his hands up. "I presented him with an interpretation of what I observed, highlighting certain aspects and leaving out others. Which is how, when he broached the idea of a family ski trip, I told him I was sure Chloe would be game."

53

By the time he got home from work that day, Chloe had already received her invitation, and she wasn't happy about it. She saw it as an attempt to buy her off. Unlike her mother, Chloe had grown up wanting for nothing, and so was impervious to bribery.

Jeff couched the trip in different terms, saying that he thought Francis might have been trying to make things up to them, yes, but also that he was probably seeking healing, and wanted to take them as far away as possible from any reminders of what had happened. Chloe asked him if he believed everything her father said. He said he didn't, of course not.

"Good," she said, "because we're not going."

That was how he learned he'd been invited as well.

How was he going to break the news to Francis?

In the end, he didn't have to. Alison and Chloe had their daily phone call, and somehow Alison convinced Chloe that the trip could be a good idea, a starting point for genuine healing. The fissures were still there, still simmering with molten lava, but with relation to Chloe, it seemed, Francis and Alison were trying to find a way forward together.

And so it was they found themselves bound for Val d'Isère.

54

Jeff had never been to Europe, had barely ever skied, had never flown first class. He didn't have the clothes for the trip, so Chloe took him shopping. He'd never spent so much on clothes in his life: a chic ski suit, a fancy sweater, long underwear, a hat, gloves, and an insanely expensive pair of après-ski boots. Everything went on Chloe's credit card, the bill for which went to Francis. Jeff couldn't tell whether this level of spending was standard or meant to be retributive.

Either way, he felt what he'd felt upon first encountering the prices on the artworks in the gallery. People had this kind of money, and they existed among us, but on a different plane. Chloe had come down to his plane, even downplayed her ability to spend, but now that they'd been together awhile, she clearly felt less self-conscious about it. Still, he wondered about their future together. Who would bridge the gap, and in what direction? It was far harder to go down than up, but he doubted he could ever provide for them even a tenth of what her father had.

A town car took them to the airport, and they met Francis and Alison in the first-class lounge. Jeff had flown Southwest a bunch of times to Northern California and back, and they didn't even assign seats. This was another universe. He didn't think he would ever get used to it. Or, to be accurate, he refused to get used to it, even a little bit, knowing—or believing—that he had only temporarily entered this world of wealth and luxury.

In the lounge Francis and Alison sat next to each other, both clearly uncomfortable about being there, being together, and facing Chloe. Chloe made it clear to Jeff that she wasn't speaking to her father and wasn't going to start. Jeff tried to make small talk, but each attempt sputtered out miserably. Francis fetched drinks for himself and Alison. Chloe opened a magazine. Jeff was caught between trying to enjoy his surroundings and feeling utterly awkward about the situation.

It was better on the plane. Chloe and Jeff were seated next to each other, and Francis and Alison ended up a few rows ahead of them. The seats were wide and comfortable. When reclined, they were completely flat. It was a night flight, and Chloe and Jeff talked for a little while after the cabin lights went down. She told him that she respected her mother's wishes, but that she already knew that coming on the trip had been a mistake.

"If I could jump out now," she said, "I would. And I hope you'd join me."

"Of course," he said.

Her mother wanted her to do what she had done, which was to forgive and move on, to preserve the relationship, the family, by sweeping her father's actions under the rug. But she wasn't her mother, and she wasn't subject to the same panic, the same need to paper over the cracks. Her mother didn't understand her perspective. She didn't see how Francis's behavior had branded Chloe at school, how people were spreading rumors about her, having a good laugh at the situation, at *her*.

"You know what she said, when I brought up the fact that Astrid was a student?"

Jeff waited for her to continue.

"She interrupted me and said *graduate student*. She was already parroting my dad.

"And then there's the matter of the show. Did he promise her a show? Is this how the gallery works? Is this how he and my mom got together in the first place? How many women has he done this to? His eye, his eye, everybody's always talking about his eye. But is it an eye for art or for ass?

"He's a dinosaur. A disgusting should-be-extinct T. rex of a man."

Chloe wiped away her tears, blamed the altitude or the oxygen for her outburst, and took Jeff's hands in hers.

"I need to know," she said, "that you're with me. One hundred percent."

"One hundred percent," he said, leaning across the wide space between their seats to kiss her wet cheeks.

55

In Val d'Isère, Francis had rented a chalet, complete with a butler and a chef. The little village was unlike anything Jeff had ever seen, tucked into the bottom of ski slopes that seemed to disappear into the sky. It was a far cry from the handful of day trips he'd taken with Emilio and Mark, to ski iced-over trails on Mount Baldy. Francis told him, proudly, as if he owned the place, that you could take any American resort, say, Vail, and lay it over Val d'Isère, and it wouldn't come close to covering it. He had taken this tack, magnanimity, as they entered the chalet, the butler bringing their bags in from the van, but neither Alison nor Chloe was interested, and so it fell to Jeff to play audience once again. Chloe wasn't happy about it, he could tell, but he didn't really have a choice. Francis continued to monologue about how he'd found this particular chalet, how it had been difficult to book, how there was a storm coming in and the snow was going to be incredible. He repeated this one down the hall to Alison. She responded with a noncommittal uh-huh.

Chloe still hadn't said a word to her father, and Francis was painfully aware of it. He pulled Jeff aside and asked him how things were going. He had expected her to be a little more receptive based on the reports Jeff had given him. Jeff said that he was pretty sure she'd warm up to him after a few days away. It had been hard while they were all still in Los Angeles. An encounter with nature, far from home, would bring her back around, he was sure of it. Of course, he wasn't, but he felt he had to keep Francis happy. It was possible, anything was possible.

That evening, they were going to go into town to a small restaurant where Francis had made a reservation, but Chloe begged off, claiming jet lag. Besides, they had a chef at the chalet. Alison suggested that she and Francis could go alone and leave Jeff and Chloe to settle in. Francis wasn't particularly happy about this, thinking he'd already won Alison over, more or less, and wanting to press Chloe into forgiving him as well. It seemed that this was his only mode, applying pressure until he could get what he wanted.

Francis and Alison left eventually, and on the way out the door, Francis gave Jeff a slight wink, with his drooping eye, an unmistakable signal that Jeff should work on Chloe on his behalf. Chloe saw it, and as soon as the door was closed, she asked Jeff what the hell that was about.

He confessed then that he had been reporting to Francis, that he had been telling him that he'd been making progress, that he was sure Chloe was on the verge of speaking to him again.

"How could you say that," Chloe asked, "when you know I'm not?"

"Will you never be?" he asked.

This was the wrong thing to say.

"You promised," she said, "that you were with me, one hundred percent. How can you be reporting back to him?"

"I just want peace," Jeff said.

"That ship has sailed," she said.

56

They skied the next day, under sunny skies and over groomed trails. Jeff took a lesson with Chloe, who didn't need one but stuck around so he wouldn't be alone, a rapprochement, he thought. Francis and Alison skied a half-day, made their way to a lodge for lunch, and then window-shopped in the afternoon. Francis may have been the one who brought them all to Val d'Isère, but Alison was setting the agenda.

Several times Jeff caught Chloe enjoying herself, and then, as if remembering why they were there, she would draw down her lips, narrow her eyes. He could tell that she was thinking things over and not communicating any of it to him. This was one of her qualities, akin to her mother's ability to conceal what she was feeling at any given moment. Chloe could choose when she wanted to react to things. Jeff was the opposite. He expressed what he felt in the moment. He didn't understand how she could put everything on hold, and he'd always struggled to accept the phrase "We'll talk about this later."

Over dinner that night—they stayed in, the chef made *loup de mer*—after they'd gotten into the second bottle of wine, she said that she wanted to tell her father something. She said this to Alison, not Francis. She refused to address him directly, asked Alison to tell him as if he weren't sitting across the table from her.

In the midst of all of this, she said, she couldn't believe that her father would stoop so low as to recruit her boyfriend as a double agent, using his job as leverage, to report on her. This, to her, didn't represent an act of caring—as Francis was saying, trying to defend himself—but an additional breach of trust that showed he would rather attempt to control her than show her— or Alison—any real, true respect.

Francis said his daughter's name. She said, to Alison, that he shouldn't get to speak, but because she couldn't prevent him, she could assure him that she wasn't about to engage him in conversation. Not now, not ever. Francis, looking at Jeff, managed a "But I thought—" before Chloe interrupted him, saying to Alison that he had been misinformed, that her anger toward him had not abated, that she wasn't getting any closer to speaking to him again, and that, in fact, since this business with Jeff had come to light, she wasn't likely to get there anytime soon.

From Francis: "I only—"

But Chloe wasn't finished. "His little spy," she said, "all but forcibly recruited by him, was in fact, unwittingly, from his desire to please, to please all of us, a triple agent."

Francis looked at Jeff quizzically.

"There was no progress," Chloe continued. "He made it up. There might have been progress, here, on this trip"—her voice broke—"but now how the fuck am I supposed to trust anyone anymore?"

Jeff tried to take her hand, but she shook it off.

"I just want to go home," she said.

"Nobody's going home," Francis said.

That night, Jeff looked for all kinds of ways to reassure himself that things would be okay with Chloe, but now that she'd said her part, it seemed that she couldn't go back to pretending that she wasn't mad at him. There was no unscrambling the egg.

He told her that he understood she didn't have a timeline for how long she would be mad at her father, but that his own transgression had been comparatively minor, and he hadn't been given a choice, really, and he was deeply sorry for having misrepresented her, but he remained one hundred percent in her corner, and did she have any idea how long she was going to be giving him the cold shoulder, because he didn't think he could take it much longer.

She turned her back to him and shut off the light.

At least she hadn't kicked him out of the bed.

He tossed and turned that night, his dreams a mélange of attachments and detachments, feuds and reconciliations, and, most of all, a pervading sense that in trying to please everyone, he had pleased no one.

57

They awoke to a world blanketed in fresh snow, still falling thickly, white flakes in a gray sky, the top of the mountain completely invisible. Jeff kissed Chloe on the forehead, but she didn't stir. He suspected that she was awake and pretending, but he didn't want to push things. He had demonstrated his love. She would come to see that everything he did, everything he had done, had stemmed from that love, which was pure.

In the kitchen he found Francis, up and drinking French-press coffee, staring out the window at the falling snow. He displayed no residual uneasiness from the night before, even offering to pour Jeff a cup.

"Today we ski," he said.

Jeff nodded.

"You and I," he said.

Jeff hadn't seen Francis ski, but he could tell from the way he moved, the way he carried his equipment, that he knew what he was doing.

"I'm slow," Jeff said.

"You've had a brush-up lesson, haven't you? I bet you're ready. Besides, we could use a bit of fun after yesterday's drama. We'll give Alison and Chloe their space."

Jeff felt awkward about leaving Chloe, especially since he had committed to her one hundred percent, but he knew also that Francis was right, that she and Alison could use a little time to themselves.

Chloe rolled out of bed soon after. She poured herself the remains of the coffee without a word to either of them.

"Today is another day," Francis said.

She poured cream and sugar into her mug.

"We were thinking," Jeff said, "that we could give you and your mom some space today."

She sipped her coffee once, then went back to the bedroom. Jeff followed.

"Make up your mind," she said. "Are you giving me space or not?"

"I'm going to, yes."

He said that he thought it was a good idea, that she and her mom hadn't had time to talk, that he could keep Francis occupied, that his loyalties lay with her, one hundred percent, and that he was unwavering on that point.

"Why can't he go off on his own?" she asked.

"Where would I go?"

"You could go off on your own too."

Taking her hand in his, he reminded her that Francis was his boss, and not just any boss, a generous boss, one who had taken a genuine interest in him.

"Go ahead," she said, pulling back her hand. "Do what you want. Run away with him."

"Come on, that's unfair."

The look she gave him made it clear that there was no point in pursuing the argument.

58

Jeff had never seen so much snow. Trudging through it in stiff ski boots required serious effort. He struggled to keep up with Francis, who talked to him over his shoulder as they walked, saying nothing about the day before, about the reason for the trip, even about Chloe.

Today, Francis declared, would be a vacation day. Petty human squabbles weren't going to prevent them from relishing nature's bounty. To that end, he wanted to introduce Jeff to a special part of the mountain, his favorite.

By the time they made it to the gondola, Jeff was breathing hard. Snow fell continuously. There was no line. The little pod came around the bend, and its doors popped open automatically. They boarded it, sitting across from each other, knees almost touching, holding their skis upright next to them like lances.

Suspended on a wire, the car rose above a white carpet of bumps. Jeff's mouth went dry. Soon they could see only the area immediately around them, a sphere of visibility that extended just to the gondola ahead and down to the run below. Val d'Isère disappeared completely. A post appeared out of nowhere and the gondola rumbled over a series of wheels before hanging again from the wire. Condensation steamed the windows even as the clouds thickened outside. They hovered in a featureless gray void.

Francis, eyelid drooping, goggles on his forehead, surveyed Jeff. He seemed to relish having the young man close at hand, his for the viewing, as if he were a sculpture or painting. The trace of a smile appeared at the corner of his mouth.

"You had long hair," he said.

It took a moment for Jeff to process what he'd heard. To understand everything contained in those four words. Above all—he was caught. He didn't know how to respond. Francis smiled fully now, watching Jeff. How long had he known? Since the night with the cigars? Had Francis brought him here just for this? To pull the plug on the life he had managed to build for himself?

Jeff locked his vision on his knees, on his and Francis's knees. He could feel the older man's eyes on him, observing coolly what he had set off in Jeff. He had lit the fuse and blown out the match.

Another rumble, and the gondola doors popped open with a blast of cold air.

Francis stepped out, skis in hand. Jeff considered riding the gondola to the bottom, getting to Chloe before Francis could, telling her he loved her, grabbing his passport, and disappearing into Europe. And then? He was at a loss.

"You coming or what?"

Jeff rose, his legs jelly, and stepped out. The gondola's machinery whirred in his ears, far away. He willed himself to put one foot in front of the other.

Outside, Francis dropped his skis to the snow and stepped into his bindings with two solid clunks. Jeff did the same, shackling himself to the two boards.

"You're not going to believe this run," Francis said cheerily.

Jeff searched his face for any residue of what he had said on the gondola, but his look was neutral, betraying nothing. He lowered his mirrored ski goggles into place, leaving Jeff with only his own diminished reflection.

Francis set off, his skis neat and parallel and seemingly obeying his every whim. Jeff trailed behind, alternating between a snowplow and moments when he let the skis go straighter, accelerating to keep up. The slope was gradual but consistent, challenging for Jeff. He was again breathing hard by the time he got to Francis, who had stopped, seemingly not having exerted himself at all.

"You all right back there?" Francis didn't wait for an answer. He took off as soon as Jeff reached him.

The air felt thin. Jeff struggled to catch his breath. What the hell was Francis up to?

Then there was the matter of the mountain. Jeff didn't know one run from another, couldn't read French, wasn't familiar with the symbols on the signs, signs that were hardly visible through the snowfall. He wasn't exhausted, not yet, but he hoped the run wasn't going to get much more difficult. What he didn't know, what he, reasonably, had not understood, was that they hadn't reached the run itself. That awareness came moments later, when he caught up to a stopped Francis yet again. The slope dropped precipitously ahead and disappeared out of sight. There was no other way down.

"Voilà! Epaule du Charvet." Francis grinned.

Jeff felt a wave of nausea. The impossible descent in front of him made it clear that Francis's purpose in dragging him up the mountain was to torture him before blowing his life to smithereens. To torture and humiliate him, the kid, the upstart, the young man in whom Francis supposedly saw so much of himself.

Jeff couldn't go straight down the mountain. That would be suicide. Even his deepest snowplow wouldn't help him here. The only sane approach would be a slow traverse, back and forth across the face. Deliberate and slow. He refused to give Francis any satisfaction. He started off skiing across the face at a slight angle, hardly making a dent in the altitude, and soon found himself at the edge of the run. He had to turn around and go the other way, but if he pointed his skis downhill, even for a moment, he would wind up flying down the slope, out of control, unable to stop. He sat in the snow, raised his legs in the air, and rotated his skis so that they were now pointing back across the slope. He raised himself to standing with the help of his poles. He tried a slightly steeper angle across the run this time, gaining a bit more speed. Then, out of nowhere, he hit a bump, a hard mogul concealed under the fresh powder, and fell, landing on his hip, then sliding on his belly, head first, trying to slow himself with his skis, one of which came off. Once he was stopped, wet and cold and in some pain, he crawled back up to the ski and tried to figure out how to get it on again. At that moment, Francis sprayed him with a fan of snow, stopping just below him.

"Need a hand?"

Jeff didn't respond. He got his boot back in the binding and rose to his feet. Francis tore down the slope, his knees like shock absorbers, bouncing from invisible mogul to invisible mogul, until he was out of sight.

Alone on the piste, cold and wet and exhausted, his hip throbbing with pain, Jeff seethed. The landscape was so white and vertiginously steep that it seemed less that the snow was falling than the earth was rising to meet it. He had to get down the mountain. He made several more traverses, fell a few times—gratefully shedding altitude while unceremoniously sliding downhill on his bottom—and made his way, eventually, to the foot of the slope, where he found Francis waiting.

"Take all the time you need," he said.

Jeff gave no reply. Francis dropped the sarcasm, like a cat giving its mouse a respite before going another round.

"Let me give you a tip, seriously. You can ski down this mountain. You just need to commit to your turns. It's a hopping motion, more or less." He demonstrated it in place. "This next section is slightly more challenging, but it's got a long runoff. If you find yourself accelerating out of control, just bend your knees and point the skis downhill and hold on. You'll stop eventually."

Now Jeff saw that they were only on a short plateau between two steep parts, the next one curving around to the right, and, as with the previous one, disappearing down out of sight. Below and beyond was only white and gray, no sign of the end.

The run narrowed, the traverses shortened, and Jeff had to reverse direction more often. To avoid putting weight on his injured hip, he tried to turn around while standing and almost ended up headed downhill. He couldn't understand how anyone could enjoy this. It was pure agony, wanting to be at the bottom, wanting to be home. But what bottom, what home?

Francis whistled from up top. He whipped down the run, skis parallel, bouncing off the hidden moguls as before. Jeff watched the technique while also recognizing its irrelevance to his own efforts. Francis was showing off, rubbing it in, leveraging the humiliation. He breezed past Jeff as close as he could without taking him out, not uttering a word on his way past.

Jeff stopped his traverse, swinging his poles to try to regain his balance from Francis's fly-by, and fell softly into the face of the mountain. By the time he righted himself again, Francis was a dark form in the middle distance, perched on the side of the run, catching his breath.

What if, Jeff wondered, he pointed his own skis down the slope now? Could his knees absorb enough of the shock of the moguls? Could he bomb the hill, blow past Francis, emerge victorious? He traversed twice with this possibility in mind, testing slightly steeper angles, his skis pulsing up and down. No, any faster and he wouldn't know how to stop.

Francis started down again, and Jeff couldn't help but be struck by the speed and beauty of his skiing, knowing that never in his life would he be able to ski like that, to respond to the terrain so deftly, intuitively, and to maintain that uncanny sense of balance, as if his head was on a gimbal. Francis was in rhythm with the slope, a master of control, sustaining a steady beat, even as he accelerated down the mountain. Was he trying to make the runoff?

Then Francis lost his rhythm completely, the moguls punishing his body until one sent him careening into the air. He came down hard, his legs crumpling under him, and tumbled in the snow.

Jeff focused on getting himself down the mountain. He returned to his traversing. Soon he came to Francis, splayed out where he went down, head downhill, his legs still connected to his skis. Jeff couldn't see whether his eyes were open or closed behind the mirrored goggles.

"Are you all right?" he asked.

There was no response.

"I'll get help," he said.

He continued down the mountain, traversing back and forth, back and forth, Francis's fall playing on a loop in his mind. He would summon the ski patrol as soon as he got to the bottom.

Jeff raised his eyebrows at me, as if to say, That's it.

"You got help?" I asked.

"I told myself many stories about what happened on that mountain. Countless plausibilities. What I thought might have happened. I told myself I'd done the right thing, heading down to fetch the ski patrol. But I knew. I refused to acknowledge it, even to myself, but when I saw him go down, a part of me knew immediately what had happened. He didn't wipe out so much as collapse. All tension gone from his muscles. Like someone had cut the marionette strings."

"His heart?" I asked.

"Ski patrol went up with a snowmobile and a litter. A small group of skiers had stopped. By the time they reached him he'd already been covered by a dusting of fresh snow. He looked like someone who had succumbed to the elements on Everest."

"You couldn't have saved him," I said, trying to offer comfort.

"That's kind of you to say. It might even be true. But the fact remains that I didn't try."

60

He looked at me, as he neared the conclusion of his story, a story I was still trying to wrap my head around, a story he seemed to have told off the cuff, unrehearsed, spontaneously upon finally meeting an ideal audience—though whether ideal because I knew him long ago, when his heart was good, as he had put it, or, as I had come to suspect, because I was someone who might transform his account into a kind of (I hate the term) *roman à clef* for the consumption of an invisible horde of anonymous readers, their combined consciousnesses constituting a kind of archive into which his narrative could settle, no longer trapped in his head, no longer susceptible to his mortality, or perhaps for those who would recognize him despite the changed names, who knew him and thought they knew his story, to redeem him in their eyes, or to confess to them indirectly, to justify himself or satisfy his critics, I couldn't be sure—he looked at me, tired perhaps from talking, from spending the better part of the day in an airport lounge, from drink, he looked at me in—how else to put it?—supplication.

After he'd summoned the ski patrol, he said, he waited. It was a long time before he heard anything. He kept an ear out for any news coming over the radios. He didn't speak or understand French, so he couldn't tell what was being said, but at one point one of the men holding a radio closed his eyes and shook his head. That was when Jeff knew what he already knew. Francis was gone. The same anomaly in his heart that had caused him to nearly drown in the ocean that morning long ago had struck again in a moment of overexertion.

Something the doctors hadn't been able to figure out earlier, because, he found out later, Francis hadn't divulged to them his habitual cocaine use.

An ambulance wailed its patently European wail and pulled up nearby. The ski patrol emerged from the gray mist with the litter behind them, bumping along in the snow, carrying Francis's bundled body. Jeff could see on their faces that there was no hope.

The medics went through the motions, loading Francis onto a gurney and sliding him into the back of the ambulance. For a moment, the sight of the paramedics and the gurney, the memory of Francis's form, obscure in the distance, made Jeff feel that he was living an echo of the rescue on the beach, and that this morning marked the end of something begun that morning, a dilation, opened by Jeff, in which Francis had been given the chance to live his life a little while longer. He hadn't saved the man's life, only postponed his death.

His mind brimmed with these formulations as he tried to avoid thinking about what he'd done, or, more accurately, not done. As he tried to avoid, too, the overwhelming feeling of relief that his secret would never be exposed. Fortune had favored the blameless.

He found Alison and Chloe at the chalet in their sweats, drinks in hand. They'd been snowshoeing. They'd had a snowball fight. Nature was working on them as Francis had predicted. Mother and daughter were making the best of things. Chloe greeted Jeff with a warm smile, then remembered that she was supposed to be angry with him. He wasn't sure how deep it went, how long it would have gone on if what had happened hadn't happened, but her grievances would soon seem petty and insignificant in the face of what was to come, a brush fire with an A-bomb dropped on it.

He had no idea how to tell them. Francis was dead. Jeff hadn't confirmed it, had only walked away from the ski patrol office back to the chalet, alone. But he was sure. What could he say?

"There was an accident. You'd better call the hospital."

A fusillade of questions from both Chloe and Alison.

"I don't know, he fell. Ski patrol came."

Where? they wanted to know. How?

"Epaule du Charvet," he said.

Chloe looked at him in confusion. "He fell on that run? How do you know? Were you with him?"

Jeff nodded.

"He took you on that run? No way were you going to make it down that in one piece."

"I don't know," Jeff said. "Maybe that was the idea."

Alison was on the phone by then, speaking in French, repeating Francis's name into the receiver. Color drained from her face and she was silent.

"They told us to come to the hospital. They can't say more."

"What does that mean?" Chloe asked. She turned to Jeff. "Was he all right when you saw him?"

"I'm not a doctor," he said. "I got help as quickly as I could."

Chloe started to cry. Jeff hugged her, and she did not push him away.

62

The canonization started immediately. Francis was remembered for his generosity, his eye, his being the best father anyone could ask for, his being an exacting and shrewd businessman, his having made careers, his stamina, his being Alison's "rock," his sense of adventure, his indefatigable curiosity, his mentorship, his support of artists famous and obscure, his aid to the museum community, his patronage, his vision for the future of galleries and contemporary art in America, his not-always-popular-but-always-correct decisions, his legacy, his ability to throw a good party, the list went on.

Naturally, nobody mentioned his infidelities, his treachery, his tendency toward domination and humiliation, his utterly mercenary approach to most art, his yelling, his firing people on a whim, his inability to or lack of desire to recognize the inner lives of others, his avarice, his all-around tendency to make miserable the lives of those closest to him.

Chloe's anger toward her father transformed into a sharp and ongoing regret that he had died during a period when she wasn't speaking to him. The irreversibility of this struck her as cosmically unfair.

As for Alison, she couldn't speak of Francis without her eyes welling up, but from the outside, her life had improved immeasurably. She was free now, independent, and she didn't shy away from challenge. She inherited the gallery, and, having heard Francis's monologues about Marcus and Andrea, did not promote either to the director position but rather assumed it herself, quite capably, turning out to have an eye far superior to her husband's, not to mention a tendency to discover underrepresented women artists, none of whom would have been to her late husband's prurient tastes. And she displayed more kindness and generosity than she ever had before, as if her marriage to Francis had kept in check her most charitable tendencies.

The Mandeville dream house, the one at which Jeff had first sought Francis, was sold as soon as it was completed.

63

"The gallery didn't collapse, then."

"I hadn't counted on Alison."

"And now you're a dealer yourself."

He nodded. "For a while, things were complicated. Alison and Chloe turned inward, leaned on each other. I didn't know where I stood in the whole picture. I kept going to work. Chloe and I were still dating, technically. But I kept my distance a little. In the same way that I had looked at everything and felt responsible for it happening when Francis was alive, I now felt responsible for everything happening as a result of his dying on the slopes, because I was convinced—no matter what you say, no matter what I believe now, which is that you're probably right—I was convinced that I could have saved him. I had done it before, hadn't I? And so I felt as though every tear that was shed, every memory that was sugarcoated, all of it, stemmed from my decision, a decision I didn't even remember making as a decision, per se. The funeral, the obituary, the articles—all me. One shouldn't speak ill of the dead, but it had all gone too far. I wanted to scream: Don't you remember who he was?"

"Do you think you were trying to diminish the tragic aspect of it all?"

Jeff looked me in the eye. "I tried to keep in mind the dilation idea, that he'd been given extra time, time which, in my opinion, he'd squandered. In his opinion, were he still around to express it, he'd say he took a big bite of the apple while he could."

"The Porsche."

"Yes. Astrid. All of it."

"Do you still think he squandered the dilation?"

He lifted his glasses and rubbed his eyes. "I don't know. His choices make more sense to me now."

"Do you know what became of Alison and Chloe?'

He laughed, held up his left hand, a platinum band around the ring finger. "It took a good long time for everything to settle down."

"Wait. You married her?"

"Yep."

"And FAFA?"

"After seven years with Alison running things, she asked me to take over. We shuttered Beverly Hills, moved operations to the New York space."

"Francis was right about you."

"I wouldn't go that far."

I tried to read his face. He wore a curious grin of guileless satisfaction.

He'd dethroned the king, married the princess, and taken over the kingdom. Did he really expect me to believe he'd done so ingenuously, blundering forward with a heart full of the best intentions? I think he did. What was more, in that moment at least, he seemed to believe it himself.

64

An older man in a uniform came over and told us that our crew had arrived and that our plane would be ready to board shortly.

Jeff stood and straightened his jacket. It was remarkable what a wrinkle-free suit, a fancy roll-aboard, and a pair of Lucite frames could do. He didn't look like a man who had been day-drinking but like someone of taste and refinement, ready to meet clients. I caught an obscure glimpse of myself in the black glass, my lumpy backpack, my cargo pants, my sagging button-up shirt. I needed a hairbrush. I couldn't see my face so well, but I knew the look I wore. Someone who's been burning the candle at both ends.

I followed him out of the lounge, gave Saskia a wave, rode the elevator, and followed him to the gate. There it was again, his hair neatly cropped above his collar. As when we had first been walking to those lounge elevators, he didn't look back once to make sure I was following.

We didn't stand long at the gate before first class was called to board. He turned to me then, looked me in the eyes with a solemn gaze that melted into something like sadness, and thanked me for listening to his story.

"Now it's yours. It's out there. Do with it what you will."

There it was. He wanted me to write it. I had no intention of doing so.

"Is that all?" I asked.

"You listened so patiently. I suppose I want to know. What do you think?"

"You did what anyone would have done," I said.

It was the closest thing to a benediction I could offer. The fact that I didn't think it true didn't make a difference. He took it in, and it seemed to please him. He shook my hand.

"I'm really glad I ran into you," he said.

He approached the first-class boarding kiosk, where nobody was waiting, scanned his ticket, and glided down the jetway. He moved with the lightness of someone relieved of a heavy load.

My boarding pass indicated that I would board after three other groups. I joined a clump of people, some pushing through to the front as their groups were called, others standing in the way, a mass of competing needs and desires, individual identities and tastes and sorrows and pleasures, all trying to negotiate the simple act of getting from the terminal to our seats, carry-ons stowed, seat belts buckled, gearing up for whatever awaited us across the ocean.

65

Berlin was a bust. I wasn't a cult author after all. My German editor, erudite and fatalistic, bought me dinner as consolation. I let him know that I'd blocked out a couple of days for media interviews. He said that he'd be sure to follow up if any materialized.

He was too polite to state the obvious, that I needn't have come all this way.

I tried to make the best of it. I sleepwalked past the Brandenburg Gate, Checkpoint Charlie, the Reichstag, the Holocaust Memorial, and so on.

At night I lay in bed, jet-lagged, wide awake, and staring at the ceiling of my mediocre lodgings. The lack of demand on my attention created an opening to think about my encounter with Jeff Cook. I couldn't shake from my mind the image of his face when he'd denied that Francis had been right about him. The smile of the accidental conqueror. Something about it disturbed me, and, even as I tried to put Jeff out of my mind, sent me mentally riffling through the details of his narrative.

Eventually I found myself at the laptop, looking him up, looking up FAFA, looking up Francis Arsenault.

It was all there, just as he'd said it would be, with one exception.

In the earliest reports of Francis's death, not what ended up running in the *New York Times* or *Der Spiegel*, but the local ones from Val d'Isère, Francis Arsenault died not from heart failure, it was written, but from injuries sustained after a collision with another skier.

ACKNOWLEDGMENTS

This novel would not exist without the efforts and support of:
Jack Livings, Sarah Manguso, Sarah Shun-Lien Bynum, Lauren Wein, Anna Stein, and Chrissy Levinson Wilson. I am eternally grateful to them.

ABOUT THE AUTHOR

Antoine Wilson is the author of the novels *Panorama City* and *The Interloper*. His work has appeared in the *Paris Review*, *StoryQuarterly*, *Best New American Voices*, and the *Los Angeles Times*, among other publications, and he is a contributing editor of the literary magazine *A Public Space*.

MOUTH TO MOUTH

ANTOINE WILSON

This reading group guide for Mouth to Mouth *includes discussion questions, ideas for enhancing your book club, and a Q&A with author Antoine Wilson. The suggested questions are intended to help your reading group find new and interesting angles and topics for your discussion. We hope that these ideas will enrich your conversation and increase your enjoyment of the book.*

Topics & Questions for Discussion

1. *Mouth to Mouth* opens with the narrator reflecting on his recent red-eye. Soon after that, he and Jeff Cook reunite, and the latter shares a story of a woman who only flies unconscious, as well as his feelings about going under general anesthesia for a surgery. How do the themes of these narratives—and the rest of the lead-up to Jeff's saga, including the narrator's memories and observations—echo throughout the novel?

2. What words would you use to describe Wilson's writing style? How does his attention to detail impact your reading of the book and its ideas?

3. Two paintings command longer descriptions in *Mouth to Mouth*: the one that hangs in Francis's office (p. 97), and the large diptych that catches Jeff's eye in Sotheby's (p. 130). Perform a close reading of the passages in the context of both characters. Is there a deeper meaning to be gleaned?

4. Compare and contrast airport-lounge Jeff with younger Jeff. What adjectives would you use to describe him? Can you pinpoint moments when the younger Jeff starts to resemble present-day Jeff? Even if Jeff was obscuring the ways in which he and Francis are similar, can you identify traits the two men might share?

5. Although the central drama of *Mouth to Mouth* is between Jeff and Francis (and arguably the narrator), other characters—specifically women—play a major part in the book. In what ways do G, Chloe, Alison, and Astrid affect the trajectory of the plot? How do they each exercise control?

6. Brainstorm some minor characters—for example, Andrea, Saskia, Dennis, and Alex Post. Fill in their lives: What kind of people are they?

7. Consider if, instead of the narrator mediating Jeff's story, Wilson wrote *Mouth to Mouth* only from Jeff's perspective. Does the inclusion of a narrator make it easier or more difficult to form your own opinions? Do you find him trustworthy?

8. Jeff is obsessed with his perceived goodness, and he provides few details that make Francis out to be anything other than an asshole. Do you think the novel makes a case for what makes a moral or corrupt person? How does it comment on the human condition?

9. Jeff's story seems to have many endings: when he leaves Francis on the mountain, the immediate aftermath of the man's death and its consequences in Jeff's life, and the novel's final line. Knowing all this information, what do you think really happened? What does it mean for your reading experience that the reveal is left ambiguous?

10. Find a sentence or scene in *Mouth to Mouth* that especially struck you. What is it about this moment that affected you?

Enhance Your Book Club

1. Put together a list of other novels that explore art, identity, corruption, and the tangled webs we weave, and discuss how these selections connect to *Mouth to Mouth*. How does form affect your reading? What did you appreciate about Wilson's approach?

2. Split up into pairs and imagine you find yourself in Jeff and the narrator's position: happening upon a person from your past. Write a scene about a pivotal moment in one character's life in the style of Jeff's story and the narrator's commentary. Bonus points if you cast doubt on the storyteller in subtle ways. When everyone is finished, take turns sharing with the rest of the group.

3. Cast the film or miniseries adaptation of *Mouth to Mouth*. Would Mick Jagger make a cameo as himself?

A Conversation with Antoine Wilson

In 1997, you saved a man's life by preventing him from walking in front of a train, an experience that in part inspired you to write *Mouth to Mouth* more than a decade later. What is it about the rescuer/rescuee relationship that you find intriguing? How did that come through in the novel?

What does it mean to owe someone your life? It's a debt that can't possibly be repaid. When I stopped that distracted guy from walking in front of the train, he offered as reward "a big steak dinner." It seemed absurd, a meal for a life, and it gave rise to a question: How many steak dinners, I wondered, would a rescuer be able to extract from a rescuee before the situation collapsed? That became a story—abandoned because too programmatic—from which emerged the drowning incident in *Mouth to Mouth*. At the outset, Jeff Cook explicitly declares that he isn't after any kind of reward from Francis Arsenault. But his protestations, no matter how sincere, can't change the underlying dynamic, which is almost primordial, I think.

The setting of the story's telling is an airport bar, lending the narrative a timeless atmosphere. How did you land on this story-within-a-story structure? Why an airport?

The airport lounge serves as a kind of secular confessional booth, the transitory nature of the place and the tenuousness of Jeff's relationship to the narrator standing in for (and complicating) the confessor's traditional promise of confidentiality. As for the story within a story, I wanted to foreground the act of storytelling itself, since it becomes, by the end, a central concern of the novel.

As you drafted *Mouth to Mouth*, what motivated your decisions about what to keep and what to cut?

The simple answer is character. What Jeff wanted to convey to the narrator, what he would inadvertently reveal, and so on. These kinds of decisions are easier to make in a novel like this, where the narrative arc is clearly defined, and where the alternating structure allows for cutting away a lot of transitional fat. That said, it took a long time to figure out what kind of novel this was going to be. The earliest drafts were a keep-everything/cut-nothing situation, and getting from there to here involved a whole lot of bushwhacking.

To your mind, how does the art world context emphasize or correlate to the themes of the novel?

It's a slippery world of subjective value and fluid loyalties, populated by snakes, naïfs, charlatans, gurus, geniuses, bon vivants, factotums, and so on, where the gap between person and persona is constantly being renegotiated. The hall-of-mirrors atmosphere is reflected in Jeff's own ambiguities. But beneath the art world's illusions and deceptions—at its core, even—we find what we might call the miracle of human creativity. Artists who achieve the sublime, who in their own way carve out a piece of the ineffable and share it with us. What is at the core of Jeff? Something equally genuine, or only mirrors?

Is there a minor character in *Mouth to Mouth* that is of special interest to you, one that you might have explored further? If so, why?

The thing about the minor characters in the novel is that *they* all believe they are major characters. Even Rafe in shipping, who gets half a line. I could have explored any of them further. I'd love to know what Marcus is up to on his lunch breaks. And in older, abandoned drafts, Chloe was a promising photographer. That remains an open circuit. More than any other character, though, Francis's wife, Alison, continues to intrigue me. I like to think about her time running the gallery in the interregnum between Francis's death and Jeff's taking over.

There are a few real-life famous folks referenced in the novel: Brad Pitt, Agnes Martin, Steve Martin. How did you choose who to include?

Steve Martin is well-known as an art collector, so it made sense that he'd be in Francis's Rolodex, and that art-ignorant-but-pop-culture-savvy Jeff would recognize his name. Brad Pitt was an upgrade from a slightly less famous actor whose real-life housesitting situation was similar to that portrayed in the book. Jeff's encounters with Mick Jagger and Agnes Martin mirror my own.

Is there a section in *Mouth to Mouth* that you find especially gratifying as a writer?

The narrator's encounter with Saskia at the counter when he goes to check on the flight. I have yet to meet a reader who concurs, but that's what you get for asking me.

As you were writing, did you turn to any other books or media that inspire you? If so, what are they and how did they influence you?

Aside from the artists mentioned in the novel, I was also influenced by the work of Gabriel Orozco, Tatsuo Miyajima, and Hiroshi Sugimoto. . . . But also contemporary auction catalogues from Sotheby's and Christie's, along with Richard Polsky's *Art Market Guide*s from the late 1990s. A swirl of art and commerce, in other words, and not always in opposition.

The narrator's relatively static circumstances mirror those of Jeff at the beginning of his story, another reference to *Mouth to Mouth*'s cyclical reverberations. Moving away from the contained

**world of the novel, do you ever wonder where these two charac-
ters end up after they say goodbye?**

Yes and no. But maybe more no? I'm not trying to be coy here, but as the writer, I'm the one person in the world who can never—barring some kind of brain injury—experience this book as a reader. And I believe it's the reader's prerogative to speculate on the imagined future fates of a novel's characters.